RIGHT GIRL
WRONG TIMING

OFFSIDES BOOK THREE

AUTHOR OF THE RIVAL LOVE SERIES
NATALIE DECKER

Swoon
ROMANCE

RIGHT GIRL WRONG TIMING by Natalie Decker
All rights reserved. Published in the United States of America by Swoon Romance. Swoon Romance and its related logo are registered trademarks of Georgia McBride Media Group, LLC. No part of this book may be used or reproduced in any manner whatsoever without written permission of the publisher, except in the case of brief quotations embodied in critical articles and reviews.

Trade Paperback ISBN: 978-1-948671-88-0
ePub ISBN:978-1-948671-86-6
Mobi ISBN: 978-1-948671-87-3

Published by Swoon Romance, Raleigh, NC 27609
Cover design by Danielle Doolittle

Always love with your full heart, be courageous, and have trust everything will be turn out as it should.
Ethan and Leeah, you are my every things.

Right Girl
Wrong Timing

OFFSIDES BOOK THREE

Chapter One

Austin

We've officially lost everything, and it's all my fault. I watch my mom place another item in one of the many boxes cluttering what used to be our house. By Monday morning we have to vacate this place because I went to the dance instead of work. That extra bit of money was going to save us from eviction, but I let jealousy rule my judgment, and now I have to watch tears stain my mom's face. Ones I caused.

I hope this sick feeling leaves the pit of my stomach. I should never have gone to that dance. Three weeks later I'm paying the price. Not only does Adaline Frost hate every fiber of my existence, but I'm also losing my childhood home.

"Mom, I'll get it." I reach for the box she's trying to tape shut with shaky hands.

"Don't. You've done enough." She smiles at me, but it's fake and cold. Like the room we're standing in.

I want to kick all these boxes down. I want to turn back time and fix everything, but I can't.

"Mom, how many times do I have to tell you I'm sorry?"

She glares at me. "You lied to me, and this is what your lie cost us. Our home. I needed you. I was depending on your word."

The sadness in her voice cuts me like a dagger. She's right. I did tell her I was going to work. Instead, I took some cash from our bill jar, snuck out in regular clothes, rented a tux, picked up my date, and eventually ended up at the dance. I sulked at a table most of the time, watching the one girl I want dance with some Mister-Freaking-Nerd-King. Yes, I Austin Reed failed to win the girl, and so my effort of going was all for nothing.

The shit I said to Adaline haunts me. Much like my lie to my mom. I'm such a screw-up. Now, Ads hasn't answered any texts I sent. Hell, I even broke down and used my phone as an actual phone, and she didn't answer. I think she blocked me. I don't blame her. Voicemails are as dangerous as drunken texts. Once you babble some bullshit, you can't delete it. Not unless the person who owns the other phone does it for you. Adaline probably thinks I'm a d-bag dumbass. It's probably for the best she doesn't answer me.

It's not like I'm in the position to give her anything she deserves: dates, surprises, and what not. I mean, shit—I'm poor as hell now. I can't let her see how crappy my life went. No one can know about this.

I pick up a box and carry it over to the others stacked neatly waiting for transport to the new house. It's in the shit part of town. The house looks like it's going to come down any second, but it's all we can afford. It's temporary.

"I think that's the last of it. We'll get the moving truck

in the morning," my mom says. The sadness still laces her words, and I hate it.

"Okay." I look around the walls and sigh. I spent most of my life in this house. I met Adaline here. She used to live across the street until her family moved to a bigger house almost on the outskirts of town.

I turn and start to head upstairs to my packed-up room. My dismantled bed makes it look like I'm going to be sleeping on the floor. I bet the inside of my car would be more comfortable.

My phone vibrates from the back pocket of my jeans, and I slip it out. My buddy Tyler Richardson's name lights up the screen. I sigh. Time for fake Austin because reality sucks.

"S'up man."

"Dude, you coming to Moe's?" Tyler asks.

"Oh, uh … " I rub the back of my neck. This is the part I hate about pretending, the lies. "I forgot. I am kind of in the middle of something. Sorry." That was close to the truth.

"Right. Who is she?" I hear my other buddy Jared Black say. Those jackasses put me on speaker phone.

"Caught me," I say.

"Please tell me you guys don't talk to each other while entertaining a girl? That's so wrong," Layla Valentine says. Oh, for shit's sake, their girlfriends are beside them. I hope Adaline isn't there too. I'm already in hot water with that girl. Now she probably thinks I am hooking up with someone.

"Well, whatever, man. I was calling to see if you were stopping by. Since you're *busy*, guess not. We still on for hoops tomorrow?" Tyler says.

I swallow hard. "Uh. I can't. I gotta work."

"Really, man? You know Rachel isn't hanging with us. I mean, if you're still avoiding her," Tyler says. "She's kind of been on the fritz since you ditched her at the dance."

Yeah, I'm an asshole for this. Damn Valentine's Day dance caused me a bunch of unwanted problems. Rachel Little has every reason in the world to be upset with me. What I did was cold, wrong, and flat-out a dick move. After I had words with Adaline, I left without my date, which happened to be Rachel. Yes, we went as just friends, but still, it was a bad decision. I shouldn't have done it. I've been able to avoid her in the halls and at lunch during school. But I know my days are numbered. It's just one more thing I'm going to have to deal with eventually.

"Good to know. I gotta go, man." I hang up.

Nothing prepared me for this moment. Not months of algebra I had to learn, not the history lessons, not even the amount of hours I've had to run for both football and basketball.

"Is that the last box?" my mom asks as we step into our new home.

"Yeah."

She sniffles as she looks around the dump we now have to call our home.

"It's going to be all right, Mom."

"It's not." She drops down to the dirty floor and starts crying.

I slump down beside her and wrap my arms around her.

"Mom, I'll quit school. I'll fix this. I swear I will."

She jerks back. "You better never quit school! Do you hear me? It's just a setback. This is temporary, and no one can know about this. Do you understand?"

There's no way in hell I'd ever let any of my friends know I live in this shit-ball area. Never. I've gotta fix this and fast.

Chapter Two

Adaline

I get out of my best friend Juliet Valentine's Wrangler and sigh at the sky. I drop my gaze, and it lands on my ex-best friend, Chase Bromwell. A deep ache settles in the pit of my stomach. I hate being like this. I don't love Chase the way he wants me to, but I miss him. I miss our friendship.

Juliet slings an arm across my shoulder as I reach her on the sidewalk. "He'll come around, Addy. I swear. Give him some time," she says.

How much time could he possibly need? "It's been a month since he's talked to me." I don't want to say it aloud for fear it might be true, but if he hasn't talked to me by now, I don't think he ever will. He dodges me in the halls, refuses to even look at me in class. It's so stupid. I get how he's feeling. Unrequited love sucks. I know all too well how much it sucks. The one guy who holds my heart has done nothing but hand it back to me in a wadded up mess. Sure, his text messages say something different, but every time I give Austin Reed a chance … well, he crushes me. I'm through with the games.

Juliet hugs me, and we go through the front entrance separately. "It's going to be okay. You'll see. Everything will work out in the end," she says.

She links her arm through mine in the hallway, and I give her a side-eyed glance. "You're just spouting crap to me because you're all in love with Jared."

She laughs. "True. I remember not too long ago you were saying something similar to me, though. And you were right."

"As much as I love being right, it's not the same. Austin and I never went on a date. Shared one stupidly amazing kiss but that's it," I hiss.

Juliet and I stop by our set of lockers, and she starts spinning in her combination. "It might not be with *him*. Maybe it will. It will happen, though. Just keep being you," she says as she pops open the metal door.

Which is what exactly? A book-loving dork who pines for the wonderful Austin Reed? The girl who can't pick a college to visit, let alone apply to one because she's afraid she's choosing wrong? Hates that her SAT and ACT scores aren't perfect but is afraid to retake them because she might get a worse result.

"Addy!" Juliet shouts, breaking me from my spell.

"Huh?"

"Wow, you were in the deepest daze, I thought you were never going to come back. We better get a move on, or we're going to be—" She trails off with a squeak as Jared hoists her off the ground.

"Good morning, beautiful," he says as he gently lowers Juliet and kisses her cheek.

She turns in his arms, and they get officially lost in each other. I would say goodbye, but I feel like I'm intruding on a moment. This has been happening a lot since they've gotten together. I am not mad about it. I'm happy for my friend. Jared is perfect for her. I just feel like a third wheel.

I leave my friend and make my way to class. I'm almost there when someone shouts my name.

"Adaline! Hey, hold up."

I glance back and watch Greg Fletcher, my date to the Valentine's Day dance, rush up the hallway. "Hello," I say.

"Off to art?"

"English," I answer.

"Right. Let me walk you," Greg says.

I smile at him. "Okay."

He and I continue down the hall, and he says, "You've been busy lately."

I look over at him and then down at the floor. "What makes you say that?"

"Well, you haven't texted me back when I asked if you wanted to hang. I also haven't seen you in the halls since the dance."

There's a reason. I didn't know how to respond. After the whole being-just-friends with Chase, I didn't want to risk things and have someone else getting the wrong idea. Greg is nice, but we don't have much in common. Besides, we only agreed to go to the dance together to help him get his ex-girlfriend Candance back. I thought it was working. I mean, if looks could kill, I should be dead a hundred times by now.

"Sorry." I chew on my lower lip. "I better get in there." I motion to my English class and then step into the room. And with a crap response, I head to my desk and have a seat.

I have a feeling I'm not done making a huge mess of things this year.

Chapter Three

Austin

At school, everything around me is fake. Fake smiles, laughs. Hell, I even pretend caring. It's easier than the truth. I've done it so long at this point it's practically natural. Only one person here sees through the act.

Ever met a person in life, and you just know they're going to be with you for a long time? Might be as friends. Might be as enemies. Might even be as soulmates. Okay, the last one is total movie-style, fairy-tale bullshit. The moment I met Adaline Frost I knew, good or bad, she was going to be in my life for a long time.

When we were kids, I thought she was a pest. She's the one person who puts me in my place, and I don't like it. The same person who has me all twisted. Seeing her now with Greg Fletcher leaning too close to her locker jolts a spark of jealousy inside me.

A hand slapping my shoulder startles me, and I blink, then turn to my left. "Missed you last weekend." Tyler

Richardson, my best bud, says. "You look like shit. What were you doing?"

What was I doing? I was moving out of my childhood home and into a house in the shittiest part of town; it's practically the ghetto. I can't say any of this, though. Not even to my friends. They wouldn't understand. They couldn't. They all have nice homes, parents both have nice jobs. The word here to remember is "parents," meaning two damn people making a living. Not a single mom who used to have a fantastic job and lost it. Not a father who decided we weren't worth the effort and left us. That would be my life.

"I was working," I say.

He nods. "Ah, gotcha. Well, there were some ladies asking about you."

The only person I want missing me is two yards away. I highly doubt she was asking about me because she didn't answer any of the texts I sent her. Besides, I'm pretty certain she wasn't at Moe's or even at one of Tyler's parties. Fun facts about Adaline: she never goes to parties; she can usually be found at a Starbucks, school, Sprinkles the donut shop in town, any bookstore, library, or art store; and she'll be most likely traveling with her friends Chase Bromwell and Juliet Valentine. Not that I'm a stalker, these are just things I picked up on when Adaline and I were partners for a history project.

I paste on a smile. "I bet. You know how ladies can't get enough of all this," I joke with Tyler.

I sound like an asshole. It's all a game. That's what high school is—one big game—and you're either on the winning side or the losing side. I plan on being on the winning side. So of course, I say shit I don't mean. I say things that make me sound like an idiot or a prick.

I stop by my locker, pop it open, and switch out books I need for the morning with the ones I brought home. I shut the door, swing the lock, and start toward first period. Usually, I walk with Tyler or Jared Black, but I don't want to wait. I also don't want to feel like a backseat friend since they started dating the Valentine twins.

I pass by Adaline and Greg, and my jaw clenches as soon as I hear her laugh. I hate it. Every single freaking moment of it. But this is all my fault. I need to remember that. Being a dumbass caused this, and I better man up and deal.

Even if I have to stomach mister-freaking-wanna-be-Rogers and his stupid sweater vest making Adaline happy, I will. I try meeting her gaze at least once, but she only looks at Greg while she walks to class. I trudge on.

Finally, history, it's my favorite class of the day. Don't care about the history bits, just the person who's in this class with me. I went through three periods of hell just to get to this one.

I spot her now light blond hair glimmering in the streaks of sunlight pouring in through the windows. I don't know what brought on the change of hair color, but it suits her. Adaline chews on the tip of a pen cap, and I swear I could watch her all day long. I know, this isn't entertaining at all, but everything Adaline does is fascinating.

Kate who usually sits between us isn't here, so I take her seat. "Hi."

Adaline turns her sharp gaze at me and scowls. "Stop."

"I can't say hi to you?"

"You ignored me for years before … " She doesn't say before our kiss. I know that's what she means.

I shrug. "Yeah. I'm told I'm slow. Took too many hits in football," I joke.

She sneers at me and then faces forward. "That would be your cop out."

The bell rings, and I remain in Kate's seat even though I should probably get in my own. I hiss at Ads, "What's that supposed to mean?"

"Nothing. Now, stop talking to me. I don't want to get in trouble."

I roll my eyes and focus my attention on the whiteboard in front of us. Adaline is many things—beautiful, strong, funny—but she's also persistent. Once her mind has been made up, that's it. Her walls are up again, and I'll need more than a hammer to break them down. She has every right to be closed off. I lied to her.

I scribble down the notes from the whiteboard and zone out. It's easily done because the only thing I see is the haunting look on Ads's face when I rejected her offer of going to the dance. Then I see the searing look on her face when I agreed to take Rachel. She doesn't get why I said no to her. She will never understand why I said yes to Rachel. Like I said before, when Adaline makes up her mind about something, that's it.

I must keep pretending. If I were smart, I'd let her go. She would be better off.

I glance over at her again. Ads turns her head, locking our stares.

"Adaline, would you please read page two hundred eighteen to us," Mrs. Dinger says.

Adaline turns her hazel eyes from me and smiles. "Yes, Mrs. Dinger."

As she reads, I stare at her mouth moving. Those lips I crave to kiss again. Yeah, my imagination is going, and I can't stop. I uncomfortably shift in my seat, face the board, and lean forward. I pretend to follow along with her words, but it's impossible. I hope none of this shit is on a future test because I'll be screwed.

"Austin, please continue where Adaline left off."

Double screwed. I have no idea where she stopped. "Uh ... "

Giggles erupt in the class. This is nothing new. People think I pay the teachers for my grades. They think I'm slow. I let them think this because I don't care. At least I never cared what people thought about me until recently. I do care how Ads sees me, and I'm currently proving her point too. I'm just being a dipshit on purpose.

"Please pay attention. Sarah, please continue where Adaline stopped," Mrs. Dinger says as she gives me that look. It's disappointment. Great. It's exactly what I need, another person giving me the same expression I've seen all weekend from my mom.

I have a feeling this will keep popping up more often during the day.

Chapter Four

Adaline

I drop down in my seat at my lunch table and exhale a frustrated breath. I thought history was never going to end. His scent assaulted not only my nose, but everything about him attacks my senses. The small quiver in his brow when he's questioning me, to the top of his lips.

Austin Reed is downright infuriating! I hate how my heart slams into my chest like a wreckingball when I see him. I hate how I practically swoon when he calls me Ads. I knew not to fall for someone like Austin. It's pathetic. Considering he's pulled at my heartstrings only to snip them away, carrying on about his life like nothing ever happened.

He's the master of this, and I fall for it every single time. The saddest part of all—I know when it's coming, and I still do the same song and dance. Round and round we go but this time, no more.

I will not fall for his flirty words, his sexy gray-blue eyes, or that dazzling smile that would make a nun sway. It's hard as hell, but I have to do this. My heart can't take another of his games.

I pull out my lunch, focusing on the sandwich not the person passing by. "Mind if I take this seat?" Greg asks as he pulls out the chair beside me.

I'm a terrible person. I should tell Greg no. He's a welcome distraction, though. With Greg here, at least I won't let my gaze wander about the lunchroom toward a certain someone. "It's free."

"Great." He scoots in beside me. I can feel Juliet's eyes drilling into me. I know she's confused because I told her about a thousand times by now that Greg and I aren't a thing.

"I heard someone's birthday is coming up," Greg says. I look over at him, and he beams a smile.

"Yeah, Austin," I say it like it's no big deal. Greg's smile falters.

"Um. No. I mean, I wasn't talking about him. I was hinting at you. Wait, how do you know that his birthday is coming up?"

Once upon a time, long, long ago, Austin and I used to be best friends. Secret friends, he would call us because apparently boys weren't supposed to be friends with girls. According to Mark Whalan, girls had a case of the cooties, and only boys dumb enough to play with girls caught them. This is when the toying-with-my-heart game started. Austin's birthday is the day before mine.

I shrug. "The office has them for announcement purposes."

"Oh," Greg says.

I bring my sandwich to my mouth. Juliet says, "Yeah, we

were going to throw her a party at the ice rink. You should come."

I pretend to be involved in eating. I feel like I'm leading Greg down a dark path. I need to set things right. Quickly, before I'm in another situation like Chase and me. "Uh, he doesn't have to," I say.

"I want to. Unless you don't want me there. I totally get that. I'll warn you now, I don't skate," Greg says.

"Oh, I'm sure Addy can help you out," Jared says as he slides in next to Juliet.

She grins at him as if his idea was the best thing she's heard since snickerdoodle ice cream. That stuff is to die for. Jared's idea, not so much.

"Really. He doesn't have to come," I grit out. Not to be mean, but I need these two to stop pushing things in a direction they shouldn't be going in.

Juliet shrugs. "Greg just said he wants to." She gives me the same look she gave me this morning when she told me that maybe I'd find my special someone. That someone might not be Austin. I know she means well, but she needs to understand it's also not Greg either.

She pops a grape in her mouth. I turn my attention to Greg and plaster on a smile. "Sure. I mean, the more, the merrier." My stomach sours, and I pick through my lunch in as much silence as I can.

Why is everything in my life turning into crap?

Chapter Five

Austin

After lunch, we're all told to report to our homerooms and not our next class. The hallway pours with people, most of them I've seen throughout the day. I'm only looking for one. I spot Adaline stopping at her locker.

I'm about to go forward and talk to her, but I divert from that plan as soon as I see Greg stepping up next to her. He's blocking her from my view with his douchiness.

She said they weren't dating at the dance. That was weeks ago, so why the hell is he still hanging around her? Why are his fingers clasping wisps of her hair? He shouldn't be touching her.

This feeling is not sitting right with me at all. Fact is, I've never been jealous. Have I been a little envious of the people who go here recently? Maybe. I mean, a few months ago I used to be just like them. New clothes, shoes, going to parties, not having a care in the world. Then my mom lost her awesome job at the hospital due to cuts, Dad left, and shit just went downhill. Now, I have to make sure my mom and I don't get kicked out of the dump we live in or have anything shut off because of the lack of funds. I've never been jealous of a guy dating a girl I was interested in, though. Until Adaline, and I swear this is going to be a problem. It's already cost me my childhood home. I can't afford to lose any more.

My fingernails dig into my palm as my hands ball into fists at my sides while I watch Adaline tip back her head and laugh. I need to get a grip. I'm losing it. This shouldn't bother me. In fact, I shouldn't even give a shit that they're hanging out. Adaline and I can't be anything.

"Hey, Reed, pool party this weekend at my house. In or out?" Tyler asks as he brushes past me with his girlfriend, Layla, in tow heading toward their homerooms.

"Might be there. I gotta check my schedule." What I mean to say is I gotta check if there is possibly an extra shift I can pick up at work. With the flu going around, I'm getting more hours which means more money. My mom and I need the extra cash since we're down to one car, and it's about as nice as a busted up scooter.

"Addy!" Juliet shouts from behind me. That's also Layla's twin sister and current best friend to the girl I'm crushing on. Yes, I know that sounds lame—a guy crushing. Whatevs.

Juliet whizzes past me as I step up to my locker. Jared, my football team's QB, pops open his locker which is beside mine and says, "Going to Tyler's this weekend?"

I shrug. "Maybe. You?"

"Probably not. You know how Juliet and I are. We're cool just hanging out and watching movies."

Jared has that stupid shit-eating grin on his face when he tells me this. The guy literally hasn't stopped smiling since he got the girl he wanted since elementary school. I'm happy for him, but seriously, he needs to tone it down a notch. Maybe eight.

"Awesome. Netflix and chilling, eh?" I tease.

That does it. His smile vanishes, and he growls, "Watch it. It's not even remotely like that!"

"Chill, bro." I snatch my books and shut my locker. "I'm messing with you."

He shuts his locker too. "It's not funny."

I snicker. "Well, consider it payback for all you and Tyler's mom jokes. Asswipe."

He grins again. "Touché."

"Hey, what's up with that?" I motion to Greg and Adaline.

He shakes his head. "Not sure. Why?"

"No reason." He and I both know there is one, I'm just not saying it.

"Right. Well, in any case, you owe me big time for that limo ride from hell. Rachel was way more bitchy than usual, thanks to your Houdini act. Cold move."

I scrub my hand down my face. "I know. I'm an asshole. I'll make it up to you and Tyler, who already chewed me out for it."

"It's your business," Jared says.

As if saying her name held a magic spell on it, Rachel appears. I still haven't apologized in person. On the phone, yes, and she said she was cool. Apparently, that was bull. I guess it hasn't helped that every time I think about doing it in person, I chicken out. There's been too much crap on my plate, and this was just another piece of the already effed-up pie. I'm not sure I know how to make this right, and I honestly didn't think she cared that much. She moves faster than lightning. As usual, I was wrong, which leads us to the awkward moment I've been trying to avoid.

"Austin," Rachel says right as Adaline looks over at me. Adaline narrows her eyes and walks away with Greg.

"Rachel, I'm sorry for—" She holds up a hand cutting me off.

"It's over. Walk me to homeroom."

I don't want to walk her to homeroom, but I feel like this is the best option. Considering she could have a public meltdown in this hall and cause a huge scene. Yeah, homeroom it is.

After I drop Rachel off, I go to my homeroom. Tyler is already in his seat, and I groan, "What do you think this shit is all about?"

Tyler laughs. "I don't know, probably picking prom queen."

Right, that's coming up soon. Annoyed, I sit beside him. Mr. Crosier doesn't care where we sit. Hell, he doesn't even take attendance whenever we have homeroom before first period.

I pull out a pencil from my bag as the intercom system blares, "All juniors, please report to the gym."

Chapter Six

Adaline

Assemblies are a death trap for bad body odor, unknown sticky substances on your rear or some other body part, and boring monotone lectures from Principal Briggs. We all get the lucky pleasure of a lecture about not one but two things: prom, which is quickly approaching, and our end of the year junior projects. I would rather be in calculus where I'm supposed to be than listen to this crap. And that's saying something because calculus and I are not friends.

I don't know why we need an assembly for the junior projects. We usually create a group of three to eight people, give Principal Briggs the names of who's in our group, and he gives our team assignments to us. All done through his office. Guess he's tired of cramming kids in there, though, and decided to do it in here.

I scan the gym looking for Juliet. I always do my projects with her and Chase, although I don't know if Chase would want to be in our group now. We can always add Jared. I just hope they can keep their romance to a minimum. It's awkward when Jared and Juliet start kissing in front of me.

Amanda Higgins and Grace Wilder take a seat on each side of me, making a perfume sandwich. My head throbs from the strong body spray scent, but I'd take the headache versus Bobby Shaffer's bad hygiene any day of the week.

I finally spot Juliet and wave to her right as Principal Briggs taps the microphone in front of him. "Welcome junior class. As you know, this year is almost over, and soon you will be seniors. The Junior Elites are working with the prom committee in order for you to have a safe and fun night. There will be a pledge promise handout that I urge you all to sign up for. Also, each of you will be handed a dress code policy." Mr. Briggs smiles as he scans the section of bleachers where we're all clustered. "Moving on. As you know your end of the year junior projects will be due as well. In the past, we used to let you pick your groups. This year, however, we decided to change things up. Create more of a challenge for you," Mr. Briggs says into the microphone in the middle of the gym floor.

I look to the left and the right to see how others are reacting to this because I'm freaking out. This is completely unfair and well, total BS. I need to be with people I can work with. Juliet, Chase, and I did amazing projects, and now Mr. Briggs is about to disrupt our perfect system? All because he wants to challenge us more? Some of us get that enough already. Like it's a challenge to come home every day and listen to my parents harp on me to pick colleges to visit. Or seeing the guy who broke my heart every day and pretending he meant nothing.

"When Mrs. Martin calls your name, please come and meet us on stage," Mr. Briggs says, then he passes the microphone off.

Mrs. Martin adjusts her jacket and smiles at us. Her dark rim glasses slide a little down her nose. She pushes them back up and reads off the first card given to her.

I zone out after a few minutes. Then suddenly I hear it. "Adaline Bea Frost?" I wince.

Grace, who's still beside me, grimaces. *Yeah, be lucky it's not your name.*

I rise from my seat and make my way down to the stage but almost trip in the process when I notice who's already up there. *Austin.* I can't. It's bad enough seeing him in the halls or in history class. At least there, I can act like I don't care. I can ignore him; it's difficult but manageable. This, though? Oh no.

My heart cannot take working with him again. Once was enough, and I'm still picking up the pieces. He already fooled me twice. He doesn't get a third try.

When I was little Austin and I were neighbors while my parents built their dream house outside of town. My parents wanted to send me to another school, but the thought of not seeing my best friends Chase and Juliet really bummed me out. All right, and not seeing Austin, well, that felt like a dagger to my chest. Little did I know Austin would put one there a few years later. I might have had different reservations.

I should have known never to let my walls down around Austin again. Especially when he told Mark Whalan in seventh grade he'd never fall for someone like me. I was too much of a bookworm, and my hair smelled bad. It broke my heart to hear his words behind one of the stacks of books in the library. Did I learn though? No. Because this year I worked with Austin on another class project for history. Let's just say I let him in again, and I got duped.

Now, I am standing in the middle of the gym floor with him, Rachel Little, Zander Hastins, and Lucas Walker. This is officially the group from hell. I squeeze my eyes shut hoping this is all just a bad dream. I must have passed out during the assembly. That's it. It has to be a perfume coma.

"Great. Group C you are together. Here is your project card and also the prom policies," Mr. Briggs says. I haven't awakened from the nightmare. Crap. This is real.

Mr. Briggs hands our assignment off to Zander Hastins along with our prom papers. Not that I care about prom; being dateless, I doubt I'll go. "Please convene over there." Mr. Briggs points toward an empty spot under the basketball hoops.

Zander's eyes are red-rimmed and glazed over. Not to pigeonhole this, but I cannot believe I am stuck with the two biggest stoners in the world, my crush, and the most popular girl in school. Someone in the office must have been laughing their butts off when they put this team together. HA. HA. So funny, jerk, whoever you are.

I glance over at the other groups and frown. Juliet gives me an awkward half smile from across the room. This is her way of saying cheer up, and it'll be okay. It's not okay, though. This flat-out bites the big one.

An elbow grazes my side. I glare at the person trying to walk next to me and stutter step. It's Austin. He smirks. "Looks like most of the gang is all together again."

My heart instantly cracks. A few weeks ago, I had the pleasure of not only working with Austin on a history project, but Rachel was a part of it too. I did most of the work, and she got to reap the rewards. I foolishly thought Austin would ask me to the Valentine's Day dance once our project was over. We were getting close like we were when we were neighbors, but he asked Rachel.

Once we're all under the basketball hoop, I say, "May I please see the card?"

Zander stares off while Lucas nudges him and starts giggling. "Wh-what?" Zander says.

"Dude, the card in your hand," Austin snaps.

Lucas sits down on the gym floor. "Bro, you need to mellow out. It's not that serious," Lucas says.

Zander agrees and takes a seat beside his friend.

I'm about to have a full-blown meltdown. I can feel it bubbling to the surface. My arms itch like crazy, and my ears are on fire. Rachel beats me to it. She snatches the card and papers from Zander and bellows, "Hell no! This is not happening. Like. At. All." She shoves the prom papers in my chest.

Zander cries out, "Ouch. You gave me a papercut, you witch!" as she stomps over to Principal Briggs with our assignment.

She glances back and says, "As if I care." Then she continues toward Mr. Briggs.

"Well, this has been fun," I say, and I unclip one policy paper and hand the rest to Austin. Then I go over to join Rachel to see what she's doing.

Once I reach her, my small spark of hope that this would

somehow correct itself banishes. Rachel sags. "But Mr. Briggs, you don't understand. This isn't a challenge. It's a life sentence."

"Miss Frost, are you here to question my authority as well?" Mr. Briggs asks as his stare lands on me.

Rachel and I lock gazes, and then I look over at Mr. Briggs. "Yes," I answer.

"That's a shame. I expected more from one of my model students," he says.

I expected more from our principal, but I'm not guilt shaming him. Instead, I decide to pull the same crap my parents pull on me. "Are we getting graded the same? As a whole, on film, all given tasks and doing them? If one person slacks off, our entire grade is affected?" I ask.

He nods.

"Then I need some changes. I can't work with two people who are barely here in school. We'll all get an F if we have to rely on them," I state. Surely, he can understand my concern from that point.

Mr. Briggs smiles. "And there lies the challenge, ladies. Each group has one person who has poor school attendance. Unfortunately, you were stuck with two, but the challenge is to work as a team. Get them involved. Your grades are counting on it."

Rachel huffs. "This is outrageous!" She turns on her heel and storms back to the group.

"Principal Briggs, if no one has been able to keep them in school for the majority of the year, how do you expect us to do it?"

He sighs. "Think outside the box. Everyone here has common ground. Find it. Use it."

I reluctantly return back to the group with that heap of crap advice. What could I possibly have in common with any of these people?

Austin smiles. "How did it go?" he openly asks.

"We're completely screwed," Rachel says then passes the card off to me.

A whistle blows, and Mr. Briggs says, "All right groups, I'll see you back here in six weeks. Off to lunch."

"We should all meet in the commons after school," I say then make my way to the doors.

As soon as I step out into the hallway, a breath that I have been holding expels from my lungs. From a person I never dreamt of agreeing with in my life, Rachel's right, we're screwed. There's got to be a way to get out of this mess. Has to be. I'm going to find it.

Chapter Seven

Austin

E tched on my brain is her look of utter disgust. I practically jumped for joy when Adaline and I got paired up together for this junior project. I don't care much for the others that are in my group.

Adaline looks like she swallowed a whole bowl of sour grapes as she passes me by me in the gym. I am about to stop her, but she's moving fast, which means she's not in the mood to talk.

Tyler bellows from behind me, "Reed! Wait up."

I turn, and he is pulling Layla with him. "Who did you get stuck with?" he asks when he catches up to me.

"Adaline, Rachel, Zander, and Lucas. Who's in your group?"

Tyler grins while we walk down the hall. "This one here, Emily, Chase, and Trent."

Layla groans, "I wish we could trade Emily off. She's never here. And Trent with his dirty jokes, he needs to go too."

"Babe, I told you if he bothers you, let me know," Tyler says.

I play football with Trent, and I have a few classes with him. He really is a jackass. "On the bright side, Trent will at least work." Rachel won't lift a finger. She'll throw money at it, and that's all she'll do. I can't complain about that because we'll need funds.

"He'll do anything to show off," Tyler grumbles.

"What do you mean?" Layla asks.

"He'll do as much shit as he can shirtless. I swear the dude has issues. He's obsessed with flexing," I say with a laugh.

Layla sneers, but Tyler cracks a smile. "He probably measures his arms every night," Tyler says.

"Guys don't do that," Layla states.

"Um, Trent most likely does," I say.

"Probably kisses his arms and has special names for them. Trenty right, Trenty left," Tyler says while mimicking kisses to his flexed arms.

I crack up. Layla shakes her head with a smirk. "You're awful," she says to him.

He kisses her mouth. "And you love it."

"I do," she says.

"And that's my signal to leave," I say. I walk the remainder of the way by myself.

Just before school ends, I get a text message from Adaline saying to meet in the commons after the final bell. I make my way to the commons and sit at a table near the front.

One of my basketball teammates, Brock Simpson, heads toward me. He takes a seat at one of the empty chairs and says, "S'up man?"

"Nothing." I give him a shoulder slap, and we pound fists. "How's baseball?"

Brock is not only our outstanding point guard, he's also our best shortstop on the baseball team.

He shrugs. "Okay. The team is going through a process. Most of our best players were seniors."

"Sucks. It's like sophomore year of basketball, huh?"

He nods. "We're going to be lucky to win five games."

I make a sour face. "Ooooh, that does suck."

It's like my body is on GPS vibe, and I sense her before I see her. Adaline enters the commons, and Brock is talking about something, but I'm no longer listening to him. "Hey, Brock, scoot your ass down one," I say.

He lifts his head and gawks around. "Grab another chair, and pull it up for her," he says.

Slick move. I'll take it. "You still gotta move down. I want her close, man, not really you in my lap."

He laughs as he slides his chair down, making room for me to pull another chair for Adaline in its place. I steal one from the table next to me. I hope to hell she's coming over here, otherwise I'll feel stupid.

She reaches the table and mumbles. "Got a minute before everyone else arrives?"

I pat the empty chair next to me. "Sure."

"I don't think I should sit there."

I frown. "Ads, please take the seat."

She rolls her eyes. "All right. Only if you stop pouting."

Brock barks out a laugh as she plops down next to me. I grip the edge of her chair and pull her close to me. Our legs touch, and her eyes widen. "That's better. You were too far away, and you know how crappy my attention is."

She looks as if she's half tempted to slap me. I wouldn't blame her. "You're impossible. You know that?" Irritation laces her words. "I was thinking since we must work together, we should get one thing straight. This will not be a repeat of our history project."

Wow. She's really scorned. I mean, I got she was mad at me but damn. She knows how to kick a dude while he's down. "How many times do I have to apologize to you?" I whisper.

"I'll catch you later, man," Brock says, and he leaves.

I wait until he's gone before I clasp Adaline's chin and direct her attention to me. Her eyes narrow. "Don't. Can we forget about it and just move on?"

I lean toward Adaline. Her breath hitches slightly. I dip my mouth close to Adaline's ear and whisper, "We're not done discussing this. Far from it."

She pulls away from me and shoots me a glare. "We are."

I'm about to argue, but the others show up. This girl is going to ruin me.

Chapter Eight

Adaline

I take a deep breath as soon as I back away from Austin. I knew I shouldn't have sat beside him. I should have pulled another chair up to the table. Distancing myself from him would have been a way smarter move, but I let my stupid heart take the lead.

Zander is still MIA, so I use this as an excuse to move to the empty seat Brock gave up. It's not nearly enough space between Austin and me, but it's enough to help clear my already fuzzy thoughts.

"Sometime today, Frosty Queen. I have a tanning appointment to keep. Not all of us want to look like paste at prom," Rachel says.

I hate the nickname. Always hated it, if I'm honest, and I know who's to blame for the name in the first place. He's practically sitting beside me. I sneer at Austin and then sigh at Rachel. "Just tell me what you would like to do, and you can leave. I figured if we all had jobs, it would be a lot easier and we can get this done faster."

Rachel laughs and points at Austin. "I called this, didn't I? Read my lips, Frosty. You aren't running this show. So stop giving us orders, and do me a fat favor and lose my number."

The small amount of patience I have left shrivels away, and I slap my notebook against the table. "Listen to me, Rachel! I am not in the mood for your shit! If you want to run this show, fine by me. Seeing as you are so overwhelmed with your hair, nail, tanning, and whatever other self-absorbed appointments you have, I figured you were too damn busy to lead and command a project."

Rachel leans across the table like she's going to crawl over it to reach me. "Soak it all in, Frost. See my face? It's perfect. My body is the same. I've got curves in all the right places. You, on the other hand, are a stick with pimples on her forehead. If I were you, I'd focus on ways to improve myself instead of flaunting your bitchiness to everyone else."

I roll my eyes so hard I practically have a headache.

"Lay off, Rachel! Ads is taking the leadership reins. You're busy being you. I've got work." Austin slaps a sleeping Lucas's back and says, "And Luke, my man, loves naps. So, please continue, Ads."

My heart flutters. I can't fall for this again. It's an act. That cute smile, the wink, even the way he's sticking up for me is all an act. God, he's good.

"I just think we need some structure," I say in a low voice. I don't know why I suddenly feel small and meek. Probably has something to do with Austin's stare on me. Whatever the cause, I don't like it. I clear my throat. "I also think it would be easier if people picked things they were good at doing."

"Fine. I'll do any kind of things involving getting materials," Rachel says.

Lucas raises his head with his chin resting on his folded hands on the table. "Zander might not be here, but we can do any sort of marketing, or like, video stuff."

I nod. "Great. So Rachel is on supplies, you and Zander are in charge of filming and editing," I say as I jot down names to assignments.

"That leaves design and construction to us," Austin says.

I glance over at him and notice his cocky smirk. What in the hell did I just get myself into?

"Adaline, will you slow down?" Austin shouts at me as I rush through the parking lot searching for my mom. She most likely forgot to pick me up again.

"I got to go."

"Yeah, who's taking you?" He asks as he catches up to me.

I look up at the blue sky and sigh. "My mom. Well, she's supposed to be here. I think she got tied up at work again." Which is the excuse of the hour. I love my mom. I do. But she is super forgetful. I think she does it on purpose because I refuse to get my license. Can you blame me? I don't want to be caught dead driving under my legal name. And I've never told anyone this, but I'm terrified to get behind the wheel of a car. My cousin said she almost took out a mailbox while avoiding a runaway cow. A cow! Sure, I don't live near farms like her, but it was enough to freak me out.

"Hey. Did you hear me?" Austin asks.

"I told you my mom was coming."

He shakes his head. "And I told you to call her and let her know you found a ride. I'm not leaving here knowing you might be stranded at school." He leads me to a rust bucket on wheels. This is not the car he had last year.

"What happened to your Mustang?"

He winces as he opens the passenger door for me. The outside of this thing looks like it's about to fall apart any second. The inside, though, is spotless. I pull out my phone from my backpack and sit in his car.

"Had to sell it. The payments were too high. It's fine," Austin mumbles and shuts the door.

He says it like it's fine, but his body language is saying something different. He's upset, and obviously this is a sore subject for him. I call my mom, and it goes straight to voicemail. Yep, she's busy. "Hey, Mom, I just wanted to let you know I got a ride. I'll be home soon."

Austin slips behind the steering wheel and says, "Did you reach her?"

"Yep."

I try not to notice his movements, but I can't help it. I watch him place the keys into the ignition, and before he turns it he sighs, "What? I know you're dying to say something."

"I wasn't planning on saying anything. I'm glad your mom isn't paying for the car." It was a rude remark, and it should never have come out of my mouth. But I'm upset. Not really at him but everything. My mom can't bother to remember to come get me, yet is on my case every stinking day about picking a college. My father is always away on business trips, or he's home and silent. Literally says nothing at dinner, or to me. Just a simple hug and "How are you doing sweetie?" That's it.

Apparently, my words were more than uncalled for because Austin rears his glare at me. His nostrils flare. "You think my mom was paying for my shit? A spoiled little brat like you would think something like this." I flinch. "Newsflash, Adaline, not everyone relies on their mom and dad to buy the things they want."

The sting of his words fuels my own anger. "I don't rely on my parents." I fold my arms and give him a glare right back.

"Really? Who bought your shoes?"

I glance down at my sneakers and then back up at him. "That's different. It's a part of school clothes shopping."

He laughs. Not in a funny sort of way. More like he's so mad right this second, he's trying to laugh this away. It's one of his traits I've grown up around. So I know the difference. "It's actually not. I bought these shoes, this shirt, and everything else I have. So you can stop pretending you know everything about me or my life." He turns away from me and starts the engine. I should get out before he puts it in gear. I don't.

When we're halfway to my house, I clear my throat. "Austin, I'm sorry. Thank you for taking me home."

"Don't mention it," he grumbles.

Could this car ride be any worse? Yes. My heart is still fluttering in my chest, and the flittering of butterflies swirl in the pit of my stomach. Thank you, lusty emotions.

Chapter Nine

Austin

Man, she knows how to aim for the kill shot every single time. When we paired up for our history assignment, Adaline was quick to throw bits of our past into my face. At first, I didn't care. I shrugged it off because I was still into Rachel. Then shit changed. Real quick. Like one minute I'm into Rachel and the next I was thinking about Adaline's lips.

It took a while to see a soft side of Adaline, but when I did, I never wanted anything else but that from her. But hard-ass Adaline is all I'm getting now. I deserve it. I know I hurt her. She felt like I rejected her. It's like she wants to see me suffer, though, and I won't stand for it. I've lost enough.

I pull up to her mini-mansion of a house in the nicest section of town. I'm not jealous; I'm mad. Mad that she has the nerve to look at me like I'm some freaking gold-digging mooch. Mad that she is lapping up luxury in a safe place while I hear gunshots going off at two a.m. Then sirens, but no one does anything, almost like that's normal. Then she wants to sit there and say how she and I are the same. Like she doesn't rely on her parents for anything. I know darn well she has a college fund. She doesn't have to worry about where she's going because it's paid for. She could go off and see Europe if she wanted to and still go to college. I know all this because her parents belong to the same damn club where my mom used to belong.

I throw my car into park and get out.

Adaline throws her door open before I reach it, and that sets me off. "You couldn't wait?" I snap.

"Wait? I can open my own door. You don't need to pretend you're Prince Charming. It's me, remember. I'm not some random girl you need to impress with your chivalrous ways."

I tighten my hands into balls and squeeze. I think blood flow might be restricted. "I'm not trying to impress you with manners." I close my eyes for a second then look at her. "I'll see you tomorrow or whatever."

She gives me a smug look. "Whatever? Pfft. You're such a robot. Are you going to go back to being too cool to talk to me?"

"Jesus! That's it! It was freaking middle school, Adaline! People do a lot of stupid shit in middle school. Like Mark, Tyler, and I dyed our freaking hair blond and it came out orange for football season. Or Tyler shaving off my eyebrows as a prank for being the first to pass out at his eighth-grade party. Don't start throwing the past in my face."

She shakes her head. "I don't give a crap what Tyler or Mark or any of you did. Once this project is over, we can go back to ignoring each other. You are the popular athletic star, and I'm the nerdy girl who has now one friend."

I frown. "Bromwell still hasn't talked to you?"

"See? That right there. Stop it. Stop acting like you care, when we both know the second this is over and you got your grade you'll run right back to Rachel or someone just like her."

I cover my face with my hands, then drop them and yell, "Argggh! I only took Rachel to keep an eye on you and Greg!" I take a step toward her and lower my voice. "I left her there because of *you*. But none of it matters because you are the most stubborn person I've ever met. I could tell you all this until I turn purple, and you still will think of something else." Her mouth hangs open, and I lean in and peck her cheek. "I ask you things because I care."

With that, I back away from her and retreat to my car. She stands there for a moment after I get behind the steering wheel, and then she pivots and enters her house.

Chapter Ten

Adaline

I drop my forehead to my desk and groan. Austin. Austin. Austin. That is all I think about. I shouldn't be. What I should be doing is my English paper on *Jane Eyre*. What I should be doing is getting my portfolio together for art like Mrs. Haines wants. Not worrying and foolishly day-dreaming about Austin, his words, and his soft kiss pressed against my cheek.

He's good at being a player. Toying with my heart. He's been doing it since elementary school when he gave me my first kiss. I don't remember why, but we just got done watching the animated classic, *Cinderella*. Not the version with real humans, although I admit I love that one. Anyway, Austin and I were sitting on my couch, and he said, "I want to do that." And I asked him, "Do what? You're not a prince. You can't save a girl and marry her and make her a princess." Austin rolled his eyes at me and said, "Duh. I meant kiss a girl. I want to do that." I remember laughing and said he didn't have the guts. Then he just did it. Kissed me right on the mouth, seizing the air from my lungs, and causing my head to swirl with delicious thoughts.

Once he finished the kiss he shrugged and said he thought there would be more. That night I cried. Not only did Austin ruin *Cinderella* for me, he also ruined my first kiss, and eventually he ruined my heart by stealing it. Jerk!

My phone pings, and I don't want to look at whatever message I might have or whom it might be from. It pings again and again. To the point I'm annoyed and finally snatch it from my desk and start going through the messages.

Juliet: WC2 my game on Stdy?
Juliet: L is making signs.
Juliet: Or not. Is ur art show this wked?
Juliet: I hope ur taking a shower, or reading a great bk n rn't ignoring me.

I smile.

Me: Stuck on HW. Sry. OMG, I don't want to write a paper.
Juliet: Y did U wait til rn 2 do it?

This isn't like me at all. I can't tell her the reason either. Austin Reed being on my brain twenty-four seven isn't normal either. At least it hasn't been for a long time. Then that magical bubble that used to keep him out burst, and I've become a walking mess. I can't eat, sleep, or even think without some dumb reminder of him popping up.

I chew on my thumbnail and call.

Juliet answers, "Hi."

"I need to get out of my group project or switch with someone. I can't work with him again, Juliet. I can't. He's screwing with all my emotions."

She sighs. "I wish I could help. We tried getting Emily kicked out of the group, but Mr. Briggs was so not having it. Jared even tried to get his dad to talk to him, and Mr. Briggs still won't budge."

"Yeah, Rachel and I tried getting Zander and Lucas out of our group too, but he said something about we need to find a way to help them succeed. As if we're the cure to help them where the school failed to give them proper motivation or tutoring."

"Right? I don't think anything could motivate Emily."

"Not even Jared's smile?"

"Nope. She laid on the dirty gym floor and took a nap while we were working out what to do, where to meet. She said, 'Wake me when this is over.' I mean, really."

"Wow. At least you don't have to work with Rachel on top of that. It's bad enough she sits behind me in history and mocks my wardrobe. 'No man would want you in that top, Frost.' 'Omg. Did I just see some cleavage? Oops. Trick of the lighting.' I can't survive another round of it on top of her relentless flirting with Austin. I swear someone upstairs hates me."

"That's why you should find a distraction. Date Greg."

I sneer. "I don't want to date Greg. He's nice, but we've got nothing in common. Besides, he's still in love with Candance."

"Oh, you didn't hear? Candance is hooking up with some freshman. I don't think she's going back to Greg any time soon."

"Really?" I seriously don't want a whole Chase repeat all over again.

"All right, subject change since you're making that weird grumbling noise. Do you wanna come to my game on Saturday?"

"Sure." It's not like I really have much else to do since the people who are in my group for the end of term project have clearly stated they won't work on Saturdays or Sundays.

"Awesome. Oh and hey, don't worry about Austin. Things will work out. You'll see."

I place the end of my pen cap against my lower lip. "Yeah."

"Don't say it like that. I mean it. I gotta run. Maybe tomorrow if you're free, I can swing by with some ice cream."

I laugh. Whenever Juliet and I are having crap days, she wants cookies where I want nothing but ice cream. When she was upset about Mark kissing another girl at our winter formal, I brought over some cookie dough ice cream. It didn't cheer her up for long, but sometimes when the heart hurts, a little relief is enough. Even if it's less than an hour.

"Deal," I say.

We hang up, and I go back to staring at my paper. *Oh, Jane, why can't I write a thing about you? Why am I thinking of some boy who is nothing but bad news for me?*

I rest my head on my desk again and groan. There has to be a way out of this.

Chapter Eleven

Adaline

A burst of apples and cinnamon fill the small, carpeted room. Jars of candy line the desk from jelly beans to individual chocolates. I'm tempted to take a piece, but I'm not sure that's allowed. Mrs. Martin just told me to wait in here, not to help myself to whatever is on her desk.

Her office is set up sort of weird. She has a couch against the side wall near her desk. Instead of the typical chairs in front of the desk. There is a coffee table and a chair. A bookshelf behind that, which is mostly empty. That is a crime in my book.

Mrs. Martin steps back into the room and smiles. "Adaline. What can I do for you this … " She glances up at the wall, I assume at the clock and continues, "morning? Sorry, time usually slips away from me."

I watch her continue to her desk in long strides with high heels. I'm secretly envious she can even walk in those things. "Right. I need to know if there is any way possible I can change groups."

"There is not. What seems to be the issue? Maybe I can help you out that way."

I fiddle with the string on my zip-up hoodie. "I just need to switch groups."

Mrs. Martin grabs a handful of jellybeans and says, "Would you like some?"

"No thanks."

She nods. "I can't help you if you don't tell me what's really going on."

I suck in a deep breath.

"Could it possibly have to do with your mother coming to see me this morning?"

My mom came here? Oh. My. Gosh! Parents shouldn't be allowed to visit your school without your permission. Heat floods my face. "I ... uh ... didn't know she came here."

I bet my mom's visit will be the talk of the teacher's lounge. I swear she is so obsessed with my future she's trying to relive applying to colleges through me. My dad is a doctor. My mom designs stores. I don't like looking at surgeries at dinner. This is something my dad will do when someone texts him for a second opinion. It's gross. I don't care about how someone's office is revamped. My mom pretends to ask what we think about color schemes or which vase she should pick. I don't know why she does this; she ends up doing exactly what she wanted anyway.

"If it's not that, then would you like to share what the issue may be?" Mrs. Martin asks. *Just spit it out, girl. I don't have all day. Don't you see this box of chocolates I want to devour?* is what she leaves off, but her expression speaks volumes.

I take a breath and lean forward. "Mrs. Martin, girl to

girl, have you ever had a horrible crush on someone?" I cock my head to observe her reaction. She sighs. I continue, "Every day you see them, but the kicker is they don't like you. For some reason, your heart is just too stupid to stop feeling crap whenever you're around them."

"I'm sorry, Adaline, you lost me for a moment. What does this have to do with the project?"

I squeeze my eyes shut. "I can't work with Austin Reed." There. I said it. I open my eyes only to find her looking at me half confused.

"Please explain why," she says. Her voice is on edge like she's heard these pleas before and isn't in the mood.

"I just did. I can't get over my silly crush on him, and he doesn't like me. He's in love with Rachel. And it's hard enough walking the halls here and pretending I don't care. But now, I have to work with them daily after school for the next few weeks. That's complete torture. Surely there is a rule against torturing a student." Surely some part of her can get this. Maybe. Now that I truly look at Mrs. Martin, I can kind of see myself regretting coming to her with this. She's obviously more in the Rachel Little sort of group: beautiful, got that geeky librarian quality that guys crush on, her husband is probably a model. Yep. Wrong person to come to.

She smiles. "There is, but it's not written in that context. I wish I could allow you to swap groups, but Principal Briggs's decision is final."

Great. She's about as helpful as a fortune cookie.

"If it's really difficult seeing them together, maybe you should send them on errands. Trips to the office supply store or hardware store. Food runs. Whatever. This way they're doing something, but you don't have to see them."

To think she gets paid to give this kind of advice. I snatch up my backpack from the ground beside my feet and swing it over my left shoulder. "Thanks, Mrs. Martin."

"My door is open any time."

Yeah, and I probably won't be using it ever again.

Chapter Twelve

Austin

"Where were you?" I ask Adaline as I take the seat next to her in lunch.

The sandwich that was about to enter her mouth stills, and she turns a glare at me. "When?"

"During history. You weren't in class."

"So?"

God, this girl is so stubborn. I narrow my eyes. "I know you didn't come in late because I've seen you in the halls." I leave off: *walking with that noodle-arm, Greg.* The boy has no muscles at all. Hell, even our king geek, Steve Clements, has more arm strength than Greg.

Speaking of Greg, he stops at Ads's table with a tray in his hand. He looks at Adaline then over at me sitting next to her. On the other side of her is Juliet and then Jared. If he thinks for one second I'm scooting down for him, he can think again.

He takes the spot next to Jared and guns a glare at me. I

smirk back at Greg. I'm in such a mood I'm half tempted to stretch my arm across the back of Adaline's chair just to show him how comfortable I am sitting here. But Adaline is still pissed at me and would most likely slap the hell out of me if I did anything like that.

"What brings you here, Austin?" Greg says.

I smile. "Lunch?" I say.

"No. I mean to this table. Don't you have other people to hang out with?"

If Greg is trying to piss me off, he's doing a shitty job. Words usually don't do it, unless it's about my mom or Adaline. Actions, on the other hand, are a different story. If he gets out of his seat, walks over here, and plants one on Adaline, whispers in her ear, or just gets near her at all, that would set me off. But he's across the table, and I'm the one near her.

I stretch in my seat. "That's the funny thing about being popular, Greg. You can kind of sit wherever."

I notice Jared shaking his head. Juliet sips her drink in silence. Adaline, though, is fuming. She stands up, latches onto my arm, and says, "With me. Now."

I salute Greg. "Ah, the master calls."

For as little as Adaline is, she pulls me out of the lunchroom and down an empty hall as if I weigh nothing. "What in the hell was that?" she snaps.

I jut my thumb over to the commons. "That? Nothing. Why?"

"You think this is so funny. It isn't."

I smirk. "It's a little funny."

She smacks my arm. "You're a jerk."

"Me? Are you dating him?"

"No." she looks genuinely offended I even asked the question.

I fold my arms and stare her down. "Really? Because he seemed like an animal trying to stake his territory."

"And what about you?"

"What about me? I was just asking you a question when that jackass decided to be a total tool."

Adaline places her hands on her sexy hips. I hate when she does this, and I also love it. It's really the most perfect type of torture. "I don't need to give you a play by play of my life."

Her words strike a spot in me. "Fine. Forget I asked."

"Typical. Ignore and try to shove it all under a rug." She spins away from me and starts toward the lunchroom again. I want to stop her, but I can't. I need to remember no matter how much I may want Adaline, I'm not worthy enough for her.

As soon as she disappears I run both hands through my hair and grumble. I hate this. Hate how she looks at me. Hate how he gets to have her. But I mostly hate what she thinks about me.

I step up to the water fountain and take a drink. "I might not like you much, Reed, but dude, you're way better than Greg," Chase says, startling me.

I choke on a sip of water and meet his eyes, coughing like an idiot. He slaps my back a few times. "You all right?" he asks.

"I would have been fine if you didn't sneak up on me like a damn ninja."

He smiles. "It's a skill." He shrugs. "How has she been lately?"

"Adaline? I wouldn't really know. She doesn't talk to me. Not really."

Chase nods. "Look, I'm sorry for being an ass. I really thought Addy and I could have been something. Then she drops the whole seeing-me-as-her-brother bombshell, and I lost it."

No guy wants to be told they're viewed as a sibling. It's worse than being dropped into the freaking friend zone. So I got Chase's beef with me liking Adaline.

"At least she'll talk to you," I say.

We walk down the hall to lunch, and he says, "Yeah. I guess." He pauses by the doors before entering and says, "Fletcher can't date her. His whole prep boy shit show is nothing but an act."

"Chase, why are you telling me this? You hate me. Go tell Juliet."

He shakes his head. "Nah. I got the right person. You care about Adaline. She might have changed a little in the appearance department. She also likes a few more things that she didn't as a kid. But she's mostly the same. Use it."

He slaps my shoulder and then leaves while I stand there trying to figure out what that was all about exactly. Before, Chase wouldn't have me ten feet near Adaline. Now, he wants me to what? Sabotage Greg dating her? Not that I don't enjoy the idea, because I do. I just don't know if it's what's best for her.

Chapter Thirteen

Adaline

This cannot get any worse than it already is, can it? I'm stuck with these clowns until the project is complete. That probably means the entire six weeks. There is no way in hell I'm going to work with this group. They will get me an F, and my grade will drop. I can't get an F. My parents will not stand for that.

One bad grade, and I'll be out of the accelerated program. I can't bear to be a disappointment in their eyes. I have no other siblings to contend with, so the thought of crushing all the high praises they have for me kills me. Being in the accelerated program means I can start college courses next year. That gets me one step closer to getting my degree faster and well, being able to start having my own life.

No pressures. No lessons in languages I don't care to learn. But the best item on this list: I'll be able to eat things I'm dying to eat.

No one is going to kill my hopes and dreams. Certainly not these jokers.

On top of all these problems, my heart decides to add one more. It keeps slamming in my chest like a hammer every time I'm near Austin. I better get ahold of myself, soon. Very soon, or I'll be stuck picking up the pieces all over again.

As I'm sitting at a table in the back of the library, I notice a dark shadow fall over me. "I figured I'd find you back here," Greg says as he pulls out the chair next to me.

"Hey, what are you doing here?" I ask. It almost feels like Greg knows my every move, and that sort of freaks me out.

His blue eyes examine me for a moment while he runs a hand through his short red locks. "Good. Although, I keep telling myself not to hang out with this really cool girl because she might get the wrong idea." He makes an awkward face, and I laugh.

"Uh huh. I've no idea what you are talking about. So what's up? I can't imagine you would come into the library to hang out with me." I hope he doesn't want to hang out with me here.

He smiles. "Actually, I do need something. I don't know what to get you for your birthday. I could go to your friends and ask them, but I figured it would be better to ask you."

I glance down at my book and sigh. "You really don't have to get me anything."

"I know. I want to."

Oh lord, why? Gifts mean something. When it's from your friends, it shows they get you. When it's from someone crushing on you, it shows they're thinking about you and want you to be thinking about them too. If he's coming here to ask me, it means he's not thinking of this in the friend way. "Um. Gift card."

"You're not making this easy, Addy. Give a guy a little more of a hint. Where to?"

I shrug. "Books. Any bookstore." *Now, go away so I can focus on my work. I've only got so many weeks to get this all done.* Did I mention I'm a perfectionist? So not only does it have to be complete, but perfect.

"Okay. I don't know if you heard about Candance? I was sort of hoping to make her jealous when I sat with you at lunch. I mean, she was super salty when we went to the dance together," he says as he spreads himself out on my study table. His right arm is on top of my book; his leg is touching mine.

This needs to stop. I only agreed to go to the dance with him to help him win back Candance. I also thought if the whole jealousy thing could work for him, then maybe it could help me get Austin. We were both wrong. Candance is apparently dating someone else. Austin is with Rachel.

I sigh. "Yep. I heard. Sorry, it didn't work out."

"Yeah, well, I was thinking maybe we should, I don't know, keep hanging out together."

I glance over at Greg. "Uh. I don't know. That sounds like it could be trouble."

"It won't. I was thinking maybe we could go to Tyler's pool party this weekend. Next weekend is your party. We will obviously hang then too."

What in the world am I getting myself into? "Um … "

"Please," Greg begs.

"Okay. But you gotta swear you won't drink."

"I promise."

Good because I don't want to be stuck as the third wheel in the back of Juliet's Wrangler or in Jared's truck, which would be a hundred times worse. It's not so bad in the mornings because Juliet drives us separately to school since she has soccer after. At school it's a different story—Jared and she are glued at the hip. So, yeah, I don't want to be stuck in a vehicle with them and no one else riding with us. That would be so bad I might actually consider walking home instead.

"Pick you up at seven. Cool?" he asks.

I nod.

Greg slaps the desk and walks away.

I crack open a book, and a voice clears. "You're dating him?" Austin snaps.

Oh, for the love of it. "Is it any of your business? And what are you doing? Stalking me?" I ask.

He looks at me dumbfounded. "Ya-Yah it is my business! You're not supposed to be with him. He is a two-bit tool."

"Is he? I also noticed you didn't answer my question about stalking me." Why is Austin so wound up? Why do I like pushing these buttons? I should end this conversation and just leave.

He narrows his sexy gray-blue eyes at me. My stupid heart stutters in my chest. "Don't act stupid. I know you know he is. I'm not stalking you," Austin growls.

"Right. Well, call me dumb. Who should I be with, huh?" I slam my books shut and push them into my bag. I know what I want his answer to be, but I know he'll never say it, so it doesn't matter. I need to get away from him.

"Don't do this, Ads." He presses his hand over mine as I grip a book. I blink and glance up at his gaze. "I was wondering if you'd stay here and um ... we could work out the whole layout of the project."

"Shouldn't we discuss it as a group?" I ask, too frozen to move. He used that nickname that I secretly love and hate. The one only he gave. The one that makes me feel like we could be more than this. I know better, though. We can't be anything. He doesn't want to.

"I think everyone will go with our idea if we present in a way that benefits all."

I jerk my hand from his. "You mean, to have me do all the work while you all do whatever. Thanks. That's so very kind of you," I say with so much sarcasm it's practically oozing out of my skin. He thinks he's so smooth.

"That's not what I said. I'm going to put in the work."

I fold my arms. "Really? And what about your girlfriend? How much does she plan on contributing?"

"She's not my girlfriend. Rachel said she'd buy all the materials. We know we're not going to get much help from the other two unless we make it worth their while."

"Our card said specifically, 'community entertainment.' As much as a huge bong for them to get high off would be entertaining, I'm certain the school would frown on that."

Austin laughs. "Yeah, I don't think that will go over so well. I was thinking more on the line of making them think they're managers, so they might show up more. Meanwhile while they 'manage' we'll be the ones really in charge."

More like he'll be in charge, and I will be stuck doing all the work. I shouldn't complain. At least I know it would be right, but I'm strapped for time. I know he always picks up his mom from work unless Jared brings him to school.

I chuck the rest of my things into my bag. "I've gotta go."

"Do you need a ride?" he asks.

"No, thanks. I'll call an Uber." I don't want to get used to his whole hero act.

He shakes his head. "You can't stand me that much, huh? It's cool. Whatever. I'll see you tomorrow."

My heart tugs. My mind screams, *Don't do it. It'll just end badly for you.*

"Okay. But there are going to be some rules," I say. Rules are a good thing. You follow them, and things are simple.

"Rules?" he laughs. "All right. Lay them on me."

"Rule one: you will not kiss me."

He frowns. "Okay. Sure. Any more?"

I nod. "Rule two: you will not flirt with me."

"Is this a joke? Seriously, Ads. Okay," he says holding up his hands. "Fine. What other rules have you got?"

We walk closer to the exit of the library. "Do not check me out, and do not call me 'Ads.' And while I'm at it, do not ask about my personal life."

"I don't agree to the last three. I'm a guy, Adaline. I have eyes, and I'm going to check you out." To prove his point further, he gives me a once-over. "If you don't want me in your business, fine, but I am going to ask you how your day is because I genuinely give a shit. As for not calling you 'Ads,' I won't stop that because that's my nickname for you."

I roll my eyes. "You shouldn't be checking me out."

He opens the door for me, and I exit. He follows and guides us over to his rusted Malibu. "I can call an Uber," I say. This is a bad idea.

He ignores my remark and gets my door for me and then waits. I stare at the empty seat and chew on my lower lip. I should have gotten on a bus or something else. Reluctantly,

I slide into the passenger side of his car and Austin closes the door.

The inside smells of him, a mix of cinnamon and cedar. I missed it. Ugh. No. I will not do this. Never again. He's burned me enough times.

As soon as he's in the driver seat, he turns the key. The bucket of bolts rumbles and growls then spudders. Oh gosh, I'm regretting this decision more and more by the second. He throws it in reverse and eases us out of the parking space, then he drops it in drive. We're leaving the school, and I notice the car is shaking. "Relax. You're going to leave indentations of your fingers in the handle," Austin says.

"I'm allowed to be nervous."

"It made it to your place the other day."

I roll my eyes. *Yeah, and I thought about you every stinking moment after you dropped me off.* Stupid heart, I shouldn't have let you do this to me. "Whatever. I'm still praying it gets us there."

"How about we don't talk about anything relating to the car."

I snort. "Fine. So are you just hooking up with Rachel? You said earlier you weren't dating her."

"Straight in for the kill. Be prepared, Ads, I might give you an answer you aren't expecting."

I roll my eyes again. "Pretty sure I know the answer."

He laughs. "Oh, you only think you know. Your cheeks turn pink when you're thinking."

I rub my face. "They do not."

"They do." We pull up to a red light. I shoot him a glare, but he smiles at me. "It's cute. Have you thought any more about the project and what you want to do?"

"Wow. I totally fell for that subject change. Ha. I am on to you." I poke him, and then I blush. I did not mean to touch him. Touching leads to flirting and flirting leads to heartbreak.

I distract myself from doing it again by digging my nails into my backpack which is on my lap. "Right. You totally got me, Ads."

Chapter Fourteen

Austin

I suck! I want to scream and beat my steering wheel. Why does this girl not believe me? Why can't she see she's the only one on my mind?

I should have never told Adaline no when she asked me to the dance. She would have never ended up with Greg. She also wouldn't be busting my balls on who I like. She'd know it was her, and that would be that.

Adaline frustrates me to no end. I wish we were kids again. It was easier to be near her, to tease her, and hide away all my feelings. It's not easy now. Every minute around her makes me want to do things like hold her hand, brush the sandy blond strands from her face, and kiss her perfect lips. I can't do any of this, though, because Adaline is with someone, and I won't ruin her happiness. I can't.

I pull up to her house on the edge of town and throw the car in park. Adaline stares at me for a second. She goes to say something, probably about to decline me opening her door for her, but I'm already out of the car and heading to her side. She groans when I lift the handle.

"I could have gotten that," she says.

"I know." *But I didn't want you to get it.*

As soon as she's out, I shut the door. I want to walk her to the front porch, but the look she gives me tells me I better not. I stay by my car and watch her go into the house.

Once she's inside, I get back into my car and leave. I hate every minute of it too. I gotta get a move on, though, because I have to do dinner, go to work, and then pick up my mom. After that, I'll have exactly ten minutes to do homework if I want to get to bed at a decent hour. Although I don't think eleven is exactly what anyone would call decent when they have to get up at five to take their mom to work.

I used to ask Jared to swing by and pick me up, but that's not an option now. No one can know how low I've sunk. I was still able to keep up appearances before we lost our house. As long as no one stops by my old house, I can get through this school year.

I've survived nights without electricity and resorted to a flashlight in order to complete my homework. I've gone without water for a few days. That's life. It doesn't care if you have money to keep things on.

My mom lost her job at the hospital as head of the scheduling department, and bills started rolling in, one after the other. At first, she cried in her room. I took it upon myself to fix it as best as I could. Found side jobs, bet on things, and anything I got I gave to her. She was upset, but eventually the tears stopped, and she just knew no matter what we had each other's back.

I pull into my driveway fifteen minutes later and head toward my front door. Some gangs are roaming in front of my house and behind it. My house seems to be the neutral area for both.

"Yo Homes! You new to the hood?" says some guy across the street sitting on the railing of his porch. He takes a hit of something which is probably a joint.

No judgment. "Yeah," I answer.

He jumps off his porch and approaches me. As he gets closer, I realize he is smoking a joint. "That's a busted up ride, Homes."

Did he really walk all the way over here to state the freaking obvious? I nod. "Yep."

"They call me Blue."

"Austin."

He nods. "I see you in the papers for basketball. Don't you play for Riverside? What are you doing here?"

"Living." There is nothing much more to say besides that.

He smiles, and I instantly notice he's got nothing but crooked teeth. "You got a crew yet?"

I shake my head. "I don't want one either."

"That's cool. Need protection or if you're ever tight on cash come hit me up. I promise to make it worth it."

Yeah, that was the last damn thing I needed. My mom would kill me. "Thanks. I'm good." Because if I say anything else it might offend him, and I won't have to worry about my mom killing me.

"Offer doesn't expire, Homes."

I give him a quick nod and head up to the porch of my own house. Inside, the mailbox is stacked with letters. Some marked in red letters "Past Due," "Final notice," and it's just a painful reminder what I let happen. I need to fix this and stop thinking about how to win Adaline. As much as I may want it, I can't.

My cheap cell with shitty reception rings. "Yeah," I say.

"Checking up on you, were you coming in tonight?" my boss, Mr. Hendricks, asks.

"I was just about to leave."

He mutters something then says, "Okay. Can you come in tomorrow instead?"

"Sure. Can I ask why you don't need me tonight? Did I do something wrong?" That's all I need.

"No. Nothing like that. Money is short. Sorry for doing this on the phone."

My heart seizes. "Are you going to lay me off or something? I really need this job." All those extra shifts. I was just trying to stay afloat, not get laid off for it. Shit!

"Not yet, but I can't make any promises, kid. Listen, though, if I do find it going that way, a buddy of mine needs some more hands. I can put in a good word for you. I don't know how flexible he'll be during basketball season, though."

It's not the worst news in the world, but I need someone who is flexible. I need to keep playing sports because it's the only extra boost I have to get me a scholarship. "All right." It's not, but I can hear the pain in his voice. He doesn't want to do this to me. There's nothing more to say. "Thanks, Mr. Hendricks. I'll be in tomorrow."

"You're welcome. See you tomorrow."

I end the call. I hope to hell business picks up. Otherwise, I'm going to have start job hunting.

Chapter Fifteen

Adaline

"We were thinking about scheduling some trips to visit some campuses. Have you given any thoughts of what schools you'd like to attend?" my mom asks while I push a baby carrot into my mouth.

"No," I say with my mouth full.

"Manners!" my mom snaps. "Ladies, do not talk with their mouths full of food."

I swallow. "Yes, mother."

"Why have you answered no to our question about schools? Do you have a list started, and it's too many?" my father asks.

More like I haven't looked. The future terrifies me. What if I get in to this college that I might have liked at the time but end up hating it? I don't want to listen to the guilt trip of her saying something about how I squandered her money. I would go to a community college just to test the waters, but that's beneath my mom and her ideals. Also, I have no idea what the heck I want to do for the rest of my life.

Normal teens figure that out or have a vague idea what it is before the end of the junior year of high school. I used to want to be a vet, but the very thought of possibly helping someone's pet rat or snake whisked me right off that path. I thought about being a teacher, but not only does their pay suck, I honestly don't have the patience for kids in general of any age. Here lies the dilemma. I can't choose a college because I have no idea what I would study. If my mom and dad got wind of that, it would be all over. They'll choose my life for me, and I don't want that either.

"You got me," I lie to my dad. "The list is so big I'm trying to narrow it down some more. There are just so many to choose from, you know?"

He nods. His salt and pepper hair doesn't move; it stays in place like each strand is glued or something. "If you need any help, you can always come to us," he says.

The guilt of lying sets in. I love my parents. I know they only want the best for me. Lately, it's too much.

I finish dinner as quickly as possible and head up to my room. I need to finish some homework as well as figure out the project.

I step inside and shut my door. I don't have any siblings that will bother me, I just like it this way. Slumping down into my desk chair, I spin it around two times then I pull out my chem homework.

I chew on my pen cap, while I gaze at the sheets in front of me. Instead of solving the problems, I keep thinking about my new ones. I shut my eyes and sigh. There has to be something I want to do.

My cell buzzes, startling me from my thoughts.

"Austin."

"Hey. Can you let me in?"

"Let you in? To my house?"

"Yeah, I am outside on your balcony actually." I hear a tapping on my glass French doors.

I get out of my chair and walk over to the doors and pull the curtains back. What the heck? His tall frame leans against the railing of my balcony. I should not let him in. Why in the world wouldn't he use the front door like a normal person? Is this light-brown haired god really that ashamed someone might see him coming into my house?

I glare at him while still clutching my phone pressed to my ear. "What do you want?"

"I told you, let me in."

"Why?"

He rolls his eyes. "Is this how this is going to be, all these questions?"

"Maybe. Are you going to answer me?" I do a once-over on him. Man, he's really cute.

He steps up to the door and says slowly into his cell, "Because. I. Need. To. Talk. To. You. And. Not. On. The. Phone."

I groan and hit the handle, so it pops open. I click my phone off, and suddenly he wraps his arms around me and hugs me tight to him. I push away and snap. "What are you doing?"

"I needed to hold you."

"Well, you shouldn't." I create distance between us and go over to my desk. "I thought you said you needed to talk."

"I do. It's about this project."

I whip around and glare at him. "I knew it. You're going to put this whole thing on me, aren't you? I swear, Reed, you're such a shit. Did you really think that if you hugged me that I would magically melt into putty and do whatever you asked? Unbelievable." I spin my chair back, so I can avoid those charming eyes that remind me of a storm breaking in the distance.

"Ads, it's not like that. I swear. I came to talk to you." His voice cracks, and my heart clenches.

"Sit on the bed." I spin and face him. Austin strides over to my bed and has a seat.

"I wanted to let you know that I might not be available after school this week. It's not because I'm trying to stick you with all the work. I promise. I have some personal shit to sort out."

I raise an eyebrow. "It sure sounds like you're ditching me."

He fiddles with the end of his shirt. "I'm not. I love spending time with you. This is important—otherwise, I would be here. I need you to understand."

I rise from my chair. "Oh, I understand." If Rachel magically ends up missing, too, I know exactly what he's doing. Not that it won't hurt any less, but really, he could be honest about it.

"You do?" he asks sounding a bit surprised.

I fake a smile. "Sure."

He smiles back. "Thanks. You really have no idea what that means to me."

"Right, well, I've got work to do unless you need something else?"

"Actually." He pulls out a crumpled paper from his back pocket. He smooths it out on his pants then says, "I made this list of things we could possibly do."

I grab the paper and begin to read over what he had. "This says 'I'm sorry. I love you.'" I toss the sheet at him.

His cheeks color. "Uh. Shit. That was the wrong paper. I really do have ideas."

"I don't care. Take that and leave."

"Adaline," my mom calls outside my door. "Are you speaking to someone on the phone?" my door pops open, and I shove Austin into my walk-in closet and slam it shut.

"Uh, no. I mean yes, I was, but I ended the call. What's up?"

"I was wondering if we could continue our discussion from dinner."

I scratch my head. "Sure. I guess."

She takes a seat on my bed. The same spot where the person I dream about night after night was just sitting. "I don't want to put pressure on you honey, but I was hoping you'd at least check out these brochures that I picked up while I was at your school."

"You were at my school? Why?" I pretend to be shocked.

She smiles. "I had a meeting with your guidance counselor." She says this like it's the most normal thing in the world. But we both know it's not. "She informed me that you haven't come in to pick up the next set of the ACT and SAT testing schedules. How many times do I need to tell you that you need a better score? She also told me that you haven't collected any information about any colleges."

Wow. Mrs. Martin is such a rat. Worst of all, Austin is

in my closet listening to every word. If I wasn't a loser with a crappy name before, I certainly am now. I mean, really, whose mothers go and have meetings with their kid's guidance counselors behind their backs?

"I've been busy," I say.

"Too busy to worry about your future?" she asks, disappointment shrouding her face.

I hate the look. It practically pierces my soul. I grimace. "I don't know." That's about as real of an answer as I can give her. The truth is I'm terrified. Everything feels so final, and yes, I know technically on transcripts I'm a senior, but I don't graduate until next spring. All these darn questions and blah blah blah in my ear—choose a school, pick a future—is really stressing me out. So much so, I swear a found a gray hair the other day. I can't have gray hairs at seventeen!

"What's really going on here? Is it about that boy? I told you time and again boys will come and go. You can't let them rule your future."

I refrain from rolling my eyes and groaning. I'm going to die of embarrassment if this conversation keeps on. "Yeah, I know, Mom. It isn't about a boy. I'll go to the office tomorrow and pick up some pamphlets." It's one big pack of lies.

"Good." She smiles and then leaves my bed. She kisses my forehead. "Preparation is key."

I paste on a smile and watch her leave. As soon as the door closes I wait a few more seconds then hurry over to my closet. Austin is tapping away on his phone, probably texting Rachel. Ugh. I shouldn't even care. He looks up at me. "That was interesting. I thought I was going to have to spend the night in here. Not that I wouldn't mind."

I glare at him. "Get out."

"I noticed some skirts in there; you don't wear those do you?"

What a jerk of a question. It makes me want to slap the sexiness right off his face. There is something in his voice that tempts me to ask him why he wants to know. I don't say a word. I enter the closet and latch onto one of his defined arms and yank. He doesn't move. I end up losing my footing and tumble right into him.

He chuckles. "If you wanna check out the merchandise, Ads, all you have to do is ask."

I am about to snap off a comment, but his lips fuse over mine, stunning me. I know I should pull back, but I can't. More like my body refuses. Instead, I press myself to him. His hand weaves through my hair, and I moan.

His tongue slides along mine, and my back smacks against the wall. I press my hands against his chest and shove with all of my might. I'm probably going to regret breaking this wonderful spell, but it needs to come to an end.

Austin blinks. "I'm sorry," he breathes. "I'm really sorry."

"I know. Just go. Please." Being rejected in person is straight awful.

He lowers his lashes then says, "Okay. I guess I'll talk to you later."

I don't say anything. I just watch him leave, and I don't know why it hurts so much.

Chapter Sixteen

Austin

O f all the dumb things I've done in my life, this is probably up there. I royally messed up. What the hell was I thinking to lay one on her like that? I wasn't thinking. Not exactly. I just focused on her mouth, and all the blood seemed to rush to my brain and ba-bam it happened.

Do I regret it? No! I'd kiss her again in a freaking heartbeat. I shouldn't have, though. She's dating Greg. Then there is the timing—it's way off. She needs to be feeling this as much as me. Next time, because there is definitely going to be a next time, everything is going to be right.

I walk to my car, which I parked three houses away from Adaline's, and get in. I didn't pull up in her driveway for a few reasons. The biggest one: her parents do not like me. They expect her to be with someone who's going somewhere. According to them, that's not me. I never told Adaline this, but it's another reason I backed off before the Valentine's Day dance.

I also can't go in for the kill like that ever again. As amazing as kissing her is, I need to prove my worth. Right now, I'm practically jobless and probably going to be homeless by the end of the month if I don't get work quick. I can't fail again. Adaline deserves someone who has their shit in order.

As I drive down the road my phone rings.

"Hello?" I say.

"Austin, the electric company called. They're—" she starts to sob hard.

"Mom?"

She sniffles. "They're coming to turn it off unless we pay them eighty-five dollars right now. I thought when we transferred residence and we paid the initial fee it would be okay."

"Don't worry, Mom. I'll fix this." Shit! We don't have that. We spent all our cash on the ghetto house, moving, turning things on, and stocking up on food. I can't let her down again.

"All right, honey. I get off at ten. I picked up an extra shift," she says.

I say my goodbye to her and head straight to the house like a bat out of hell. I cross the railroad tracks which is the divide between the good, middle class/upper-class community to the dirt poor.

Ten minutes later I pull up to my house. It's rundown with broken shutters, peeled light green siding, and missing shingles from the roof. There are holes in our porch due to rotting wood pieces, but we can't do much about it. We've notified the landlord, but he doesn't give a damn. He just wants his rent by the end of the month.

I pace the living room while on the phone with the

electric company. I hate being poor. I hate living here in this shithole. I really hate when someone on the other end of the phone acts like they know what you are going through or is an asshole.

"Yeah, I understand. Is there any way you can extend it until next week? I get paid Friday. Please," I beg into the phone to the electric company.

"Sir, I'm sorry we can't do that."

I'm losing my patience. I want to break something. It won't solve the problem I'm currently having, but it would make me feel better. "So, there is literally nothing you can do?"

"Sir, I understand your frustration, but you are past due. If we don't have the minimum of eighty-five dollars today, then we have to turn off your service."

I run my hand through my hair as I take another ragged breath. This can't happen again. I squeeze my eyes shut. I told my mom I would take care of this.

"Can you give me a few hours?" I ask.

"We will be there at nine in the morning. That's when the crew is scheduled to come to terminate the service."

"Okay. Thanks." I want to say "For nothing," but I don't think my attitude is helping. This is exactly why I should have never gone to that dance. My shitty choices are coming back to bite me in the butt.

I hang up and try to think. Where the hell am I going to come up with the money I need before nine in the morning?

"Tyler, I swear I'm going to pay you back."

Tyler stares at me for a second then shrugs. "Man, I told you to quit betting on dumb shit. It's not worth it."

I nod. Yep. I fed him a bullshit story because as much as I like my best friend, I don't need him feeling sorry for me. Pity is one thing I can't take right now. Him looking at me like I'm an idiot, that I can handle. "You're right. Thanks a million. You know I think those clowns at the club cheated. But whatever."

He slaps my shoulder. "I told you those Blackhawk jackasses will do that shit. Anyway, I know how you can make this up to me." He hands me over the money I need. "After my party this weekend you're going to help clean up."

"Yeah, okay." Damn. Now I'm going to have to come.

My phone rings in my pocket, and I think, *Who the hell else can possibly ruin my already shitball of a day now.*

"Hello."

"Honey, I guess Gary and I got our wires crossed, I work more hours tomorrow, not tonight. Can you come by and pick me up?"

"Yeah. I can do that. Be there in a little bit."

"Thanks, honey."

I hang up and look over at Tyler. "It was my mom. Thanks again, man. If you need me to do anything else, let me know."

"Seriously, no problem."

I shake my head. "Nah, I owe you."

Tyler walks around his outdoor pool and follows me to the driveway. "I'm telling you, you gotta stop with the I-owe-you shit. You think I'm going to miss that money? I'm not."

I hate sponging off my friends. He knows it too. Whenever we were out for football or on the weekends hanging and I was short on cash, Tyler would always pay. He'd tell me I could get him on the next one, but I haven't paid him for those meals. Shit, and with me gonna be out of a job, I don't know when I'll be able to.

"Tyler!" his father calls from the front door.

Tyler rolls his eyes. "And now I get to deal with Captain Asshole."

I glance over at Tyler's dad for a second. He's swaying a little, which means he's been drinking. Tyler rarely says anything, but I think this is why he hardly drinks at his own parties.

We bump fists, and I get into my car. I drive over to Gary's diner where my mom works.

Ten minutes later I spot my mom outside the diner. She looks sad, and I feel like it's all my fault. Mostly because it is. She's probably worried about the electric bill.

"Mom, what's wrong?" I say as I exit the car and step up to her.

She wipes her fingers under her eyes. "Nothing, honey. I promise."

I hug her tight. "It's going to be okay. I got the money we needed." I don't tell her how. She loathes handouts as much as I do.

She sniffles. "You're a good kid."

I walk her over to the passenger side and open the door. After she's in the car, I get in and take off. I inhale and say, "I gotta get another job." I don't want to stress her out any more than I have to, but I need her to know.

My mom starts to sob a little more. "I never wanted this kind of life for you, Austin."

"I know." I shrug. "It's okay, though."

She shakes her head. "It's not. You don't get to go on dates with pretty girls, hang out with your friends, or get into trouble like a normal kid, and I'm so sorry for that."

I turn down a street and sigh. "It's not your fault. It's Dad's."

She remains silent. I never mention that jackass to her. I barely acknowledge he was alive. But the truth is, he deserted us and left us to fend for ourselves. Mom rarely talks about him. Doesn't even try to reflect back on a good memory of him probably because that douche tainted every good experience the moment he disappeared.

"He called me the other day."

"Who did?" I ask as I glance over at her. She frowns.

"Your father."

I grip the steering wheel harder. My knuckles turn white. "Did you hang up on him? He doesn't even deserve to hear you breathe, Mom."

"I didn't. I thought about it. He asked about you."

That pisses me off more. "He doesn't need to know about me. Not a thing. Next time he calls, tell him I died or some shit."

"Austin! Watch your mouth. We might be poor as dirt, but we don't talk like uncivilized animals. Do you hear me?"

"Yes, Mom." I pull up to our house.

After I get the door for her, she says, "Maybe we should consider moving to a bigger city?"

"I'm not leaving school. I've worked too hard. They won't

let me play football or basketball. I'll have to sit out my senior year. No. We can think of something else."

I better think of something quick. I can't have my mom thinking about uprooting me from my friends and Adaline. I won't. I gotta figure something out and fast. What am I going to do, though?

Chapter Seventeen

Adaline

Between the switch from third to fourth period, I'm walking down the hall, and a person slams right into my side and tackles me to the ground. My hip hits the surface, and my art materials fly out of hands and into oncoming traffic. Pain shoots up my leg, and I groan.

"Shit. I'm sorry. Ads, are you okay?" Austin asks.

"I will be once you get off of me," I say. Although I'm not sure that's quite true.

He locks his fingers around my waist and hoists me up. I dust off my pants and the side of my *I'm a book lover* t-shirt. "Thanks," I say.

"Here, let me help you," he says as he starts retrieving my art pieces from the floor.

People still cram the hallway. He's huddled near a set of lockers fetching my things. I'm scanning the hall for items that got kicked away from us. I spot two. This serves me right for not carrying a backpack as usual.

I'm halfway to the first item when I hear my name, "Adaline."

I turn, and it's Chase. Chase hasn't spoken to me since I rejected his offer on taking me to the Valentine's Day dance. He's my best friend, well, I'm not certain about that title now. He had a huge crush on me, which I was not aware of until he asked me to the dance.

"Hey. How are you?" I ask.

"Could ask you the same. I just saw Reed knock you over. Are you okay?"

I smile. "I'm fine. I just need to get my art things."

He nods his blond head. "I think there are some markers over there." He points to a pack on the floor near the trash can.

I walk over to it and pick it up. I turn to say thanks, but he disappears. I sigh, grab the other item near the markers, and head back to Austin. The tardy bell rings just as I reach him.

"Great," I grumble.

Austin frowns. "This is all my fault. Hold on. Maybe I can get us some passes."

I shake my head. "No. I'm already late. If you can't find us any, then I'll be in even more trouble."

"At least we're heading in the same direction." He hands over my sketches but pauses on one of them. It's one I did of him when he was in my room and we were working on our history project together. I memorized the lighting and his facial expression. As soon as he left I sketched it all out.

"What's this?" he asks.

I snatch it from him as my cheeks heat. "Nothing." I start down the hall.

"Doesn't look like nothing. That was me."

"No, it wasn't." I pick up my pace and stuff the page at the bottom of my pile so he can't look at it.

"Yes, it was."

I roll my eyes. "You're so full of yourself. Why would I want to draw you?"

His mouth is near my ear when he says, "Besides being hot, I have not a clue." I turn a glare at him, and he smirks. "Why would you draw me?"

"I wouldn't." At least not now. I step into our history class. Mrs. Dinger pauses with her pointer directly on the board and gives us a look.

"Mr. Reed. Miss Frost. I'm so happy you could join us. As you know, class started two minutes ago. I'll see you both after school. Go take your seats."

I walk over to my desk near the window, four seats back, and slump down. Rachel sits behind me in this class. She sighs constantly, to the point that it's annoying. One time I made the mistake of asking her what her problem was, and she listed out all my flaws. From my so-called hair full of split ends to my height.

"The janitor's closet is closer if you were looking for a place to get some quick action in and still be on time to class," she whispers.

I turn in my seat and sneer. "That's information I don't need nor want to know. Thanks."

She shrugs. "You look like you need some help in that department."

"If I did, you're the last person I'd ask."

"Suit yourself. But if you're trying to hook up with someone like Austin, you might want to rethink that wardrobe."

I turn back around. A headache is forming from her piddling perspective of me. Even if some of her comments might be true. Not that part where I need a hookup, whatever, but getting someone like Austin to notice me isn't going to come wearing geeky t-shirts. That's if I wanted to win over someone like Austin.

Last night after our kiss, I might have thought about it. Then he said he was sorry. That eliminated every possibility for me. He either wanted me, or he didn't. I certainly didn't need him apologizing for placing an earth-shattering kiss on my lips.

I rub my temples. I wish I had my bag with me. I'd take some Tylenol right this second. Why on earth I thought it was a better idea to leave it in my locker for the morning classes is beyond me. I do know I will never make that mistake again.

"Miss Frost, can you tell me the triggers that caused World War I and World War II?"

I blink at the blank notebook in front of me and then look up at Mrs. Dinger. I know this. I do. My mind, though, is not working. I lower my forehead to my desk and swallow. Think. Think. Think.

"Adaline?" she asks.

I raise my head and take a breath. "Yes. I'm sorry. I can't remember."

"Please listen to me instead of conversing with Miss Little from now on. I'm not up here because I need to know this information. Everything I'm talking about will be on your exam."

Great. Now, she thinks I'm slacking in her class. I hope

she doesn't report this to Mrs. Martin and screw my chances to take college classes next year. There are only twenty of us who get that opportunity. As long as I get this project done, I'll be one of them. My mom will flip her lid if I'm not.

I nod because there is nothing more I can say to Mrs. Dinger.

Mrs. Dinger shifts toward the board and begins writing more items down. I jot down what's on the board until a piece of wadded-up paper lands right on my notebook. I look around the room. My eyes land on Austin. He scratches his head while looking down at his desk then darts a glance at me. He motions with his eyes toward the wadded paper on my desk.

I shake my head and move the paper to the corner. Part of me wants to unfold it and see what's on it. I can't. I need to pay attention. I'm already in enough trouble, and I can't afford anymore.

I continue writing.

Another piece of paper lands on my desk.

I shove it aside. What the hell is his problem? Can he not see that I'm taking notes? He might not care about his grades, but I do.

It's not until the fifth one that I lose my patience. I uncoil it and read, "These are going to keep coming until you open one."

I glare at him then flip him the bird.

He snickers. Snickers. I've never wanted to hit someone so much in all my life. Why does he think this is funny?

I ignore him. That's right; I don't have to put up with this crap. *Toss your papers at me. I hope you get in trouble.*

Soon enough, another paper ball skidders across my desk.

"Oh my God, will you read those damn things! I can't take notes if all I see is airplanes soaring past my face," Katie Moss, the girl who sits between Austin and me snaps.

I want to correct her and say they're paper balls *not* airplanes. I keep my comment to myself. "I'm sorry," I say.

I unravel all the balls and read each one. One crumpled up piece says sorry about detention. Another asks if he can take me home. The rest is just telling me more of these things will come until I answer him.

I place my answer on the one paper and toss it back over to him. It misses his desk and lands on Trent Fuller's.

Trent winks at me and opens up the paper. Oh gosh. I sink in my seat as my cheeks flame. I hear his high pitch chuckle and then Austin's low grumble, "Give me that!"

"Bro, she sent it to me. Of course, I'll give you a ride, baby," Trent says.

I refuse to look over at the scene unfolding. If I ignore it, it's not happening. Right?

Chapter Eighteen

Austin

I slap the note from Trent's hand and snap. "That's mine! She's not going anywhere with you."

"Chill, Reed, I was just messing. Frost, you know where to find me when you want a little something extra in your life."

That does it. I push out of my desk at the same time Mrs. Dinger is screaming at us to control ourselves. I don't. I grab Trent in a headlock and scream, "Apologize!"

Trent wiggles out of my lock and takes a swing. He lands a punch in my gut.

Suddenly arms lock around me, and I'm being pulled away. Trent is jerked back too. Mrs. Dinger stands in front of us yelling, "I don't tolerate interruptions in my classroom of any kind. We're going straight to the office all three of you."

"Three?" I repeat.

"Miss Frost will be joining. Let's go. Gather your things," Mrs. Dinger says. "Daniel, you're in charge until I get back."

I look over at Adaline, and she's more than ticked off. If looks could kill, I'd be on fire right this instant.

"I'm sorry," I whisper to her for I swear has to be the millionth time. Her arms remain folded while her stare is straight ahead. Adaline won't even look at me.

"Ads, please."

She is like a trained mercenary. Stone cold, making no eye contact with me at all. All I want to do is hug her. Kiss her. Something to snap her out of this. I can't stand the silent treatment.

"Miss Frost," Mrs. Appleton says from her desk.

"Yes?" Adaline says.

"Principal Briggs will see you now."

Adaline leaves, not even a glare in my direction. Nothing. It's as if I'm invisible to her. I can't believe how far in the hole I've gotten. I'm pretty certain she won't let me take her home.

As she walks toward the door, Trent exits. God, I want to hit him. He grins my way and strolls past me, out of the office. I should chase him down and give him a proper beat-down for what he said to Adaline. I don't care if he's one the best distance runners in our school or not. He's a freaking tool in my book.

"Hey, brah," Ryder Jones says. He's a sophomore and on the football team. Usually plays backup corner, but that'll change next year 'cause Quincy graduates, so the position will be Ryder's. That's if he sticks with football. A lot of kids don't 'cause they don't like being second string their sophomore year.

I nod to Ryder. "S'up?"

"Dropping this crap off for Mrs. Ford."

He has a box in hand that looks like it's loaded with books, but I'm not sure. "What are you doing in here?"

"Defending some girl's honor."

Ryder shakes his head. "Yeah, I learned that lesson a while ago if it's not your girl, leave it be." He turns and walks over to Mrs. Appleton's desk, drops off the box, and comes back over to me. "See you later, Reed."

"Later, Jones." All I think is, *What the heck does he mean if it's not your girl, leave it be?* Shouldn't everyone have the same type of respect? Don't get me wrong, I've said some shit. Told Tyler to walk away from something if he wasn't tapping it. Because that's what guys do. They talk bullshit. May have said something similar to Jared, and he may have threatened to knock my teeth out.

Both of them were ready to beat me senseless, though, and both of those girls weren't theirs yet. Call me crazy, but I kind of think Jones is wrong—it's not if the girl's yours or not, it's if she's the right girl. Adaline is the right girl. I might not even win her over, but I'll be damned if I listen to someone talk shit to her or degrade her around me.

"Mr. Reed? You're up," Mrs. Appleton says.

"Great."

I've been in the office twice in my life. Once because they sent my schedule to the wrong address, and I had to update some forms. This will be the second time. I've never been in trouble. I have hardly been a fight. Three maybe, but all of those were at work or off school property.

So being here, well, this is new. I don't think I like it.

Adaline slips out of the room and enters the office area. Her eyes find mine, and she narrows hers.

Crap. This is not good. Not good at all.

I enter Principal Briggs's office and take a seat. Mrs. Dinger watches me for a moment then says, "Mr. Reed is usually a great student. No outbursts or disruptions, but today, as you know, he was physical with one of the students."

"Mr. Reed, is there anything you'd like to say?" Principal Briggs says.

I should shake my head. I should just let this all blow over. I mean, how many facts can I put forth here. Two people already told their side of the story. If Adaline told them how I bugged her with flying paper balls, my defense will seem pointless. "I wanted to know if Adaline needed a ride home since I got her detention. She doesn't have a license, and I don't have any other classes with her." I don't mention that I see her in lunch because they don't need to know that.

Principal Briggs nods. I continue, "Adaline was returning my message, but it landed on Trent's desk. He said some lewd comment about Adaline. I wanted him to apologize."

"We got most of the same facts from both parties. I'm not saying what he said was correct, but you can't just take matters in your own hands. We have policies in place for things like this. Do I make myself clear?"

I nod.

"You all will have detention after school for the next three days."

"All of us? Adaline didn't do anything wrong. Please, don't give her detention."

He folds his arms and leans back in his seat. "Do you agree with this, Mrs. Dinger?"

I glance at Mrs. Dinger, and she sighs. "Very well, I will let Miss Frost know she only has detention for today."

"Thank you, Mrs. Dinger. Thank you, Principal Briggs." I rise from my seat. "This won't happen again."

"It better not. Next time I'll bring both of your coaches in here, and they'll figure out a punishment for you. Rumor has it Coach Black loves giving out laps while Coach Samson likes to hand out janitorial duties on top of detention," Principal Briggs says.

I don't mind laps, but I've seen the boy's locker rooms in the basketball gym, weight room, and natatorium, and all of them are disgusting. Some worse than a gas station bathroom in the dirtiest city anyone can imagine. Like, whoever decided they can't flush a toilet after dropping a load or missing a urinal completely and just peeing on the floor? That is what some of the guys in our school do. Don't get me wrong, I belch and fart and do other disgusting things, but peeing on the floor or not flushing is not them.

I leave the office feeling a little bit better that I at least got Adaline out of a few detentions. Maybe it'll be enough to sway her into letting me give her a ride home.

Chapter Nineteen

Adaline

I cannot believe I have detention. Not one but three because of that moron and his antics. He's such bad news. My dumb heart doesn't listen, though; nope, it hammers hard in my chest every time I'm around him.

As I head to lunch in a way fouler mood, I spot Chase rounding a corner. I miss him. I want to say something like "Hi," or "Wait up," but I can't. My words are trapped in my chest, and I hate this.

I trail behind him a good ten feet or more. It's not until we reach the stairwell and he looks up and notices me. He smirks then quickly changes his expression to a grim line. "Hey," Austin pants beside me. I quickly move past him, putting more pep in my step, if you will.

I know it's useless because well, he's way quicker than I am. I positively loathe running, and that's all Austin does is run. Football and basketball. He used to be in track, back in middle school, but he gave that up as soon as we entered high school.

"Ads wait," he says. "Please. I have something to tell you."

I whip around on the landing and glare. "What could you possibly say to me that you hadn't already? I get you're sorry, but I'm still mad. It's like you have no regards to my feelings at all. And you know what? That's fine because I guess little ice queens like me don't have feelings. But I do, and you suck!"

His jaw unhinges, and he stammers, "I n-never said that." I shoot him a look. "All right, back in middle school, but I didn't mean it. I never meant it. You know that. This isn't what I've come to tell you anyway. I came to say—"

"I don't want to hear it. Just please, leave me alone. You've done enough. I just, I can't take anymore." I spin around and walk away. He doesn't stop me either.

I take a seat at my usual lunch table, and I'm feeling on edge. Jared has joined our table. Not that I don't mind this new development, but now I can't talk to Juliet without Jared hearing everything. And that ticks me off.

I shouldn't be upset. I should be happy for her. I am happy, but it feels like I'm losing my other best friend too. And that frankly blows. There are no more library nights. There are no more ice cream talks. Nope. Lately, Juliet has been spending a lot of time with Jared, or as much as she can with his schedule and hers. Now with them working on the junior project together, well, that really leaves us with no girl time whatsoever.

She looks over at me and smiles, "Hey. How was your morning so far?"

"It was the worst morning of my life." I pull out my lunch from my backpack that I retrieved after my visit with the principal and dart my focus up to catch Austin strolling past our table. "All due to someone I'm not even naming right this second," I say as my glare sets on Austin.

Juliet looks around the lunch room and then back at me. "Okay, what happened? Does it have to do with the end of the year project?"

"Nope." I take a bite out of my turkey sandwich.

Jared pecks Juliet's cheek. "Be right back. Do you two need anything at the vending machines?"

"I'm good, how about you, Addy? Want Jared to get you something?" Juliet asks.

I pull some money from my bag and slide it over to him. "Can you get me a Pepsi?"

"Sure." He takes the money and walks away.

As soon as he's out of earshot, I snap. "I can't work with Austin. I can't do it, Juliet. He got me four days worth of detention. He's the most selfish dipwad to ever walk the face of this earth. God forbid him to ask me a question using a phone like a normal person or, better yet, wait until after class to ask me if I need a ride. No. That moron had to launch paper at me like a monkey!"

Juliet gives me a worried look. "I'm sorry. That really sucks, Addy. Do you need a ride after? I might be able to do that, depending on what time practice ends today. I think we're going to be outside instead of in the gym. Weather is nicer today than last week."

I shake my head. "I can't keep being this friend either. The one who constantly needs a ride off of you or Chase. Well, not Chase anymore since he doesn't talk to me."

"He'll come around. He's adjusting. He's heartbroken."

I frown. "I know. So am I. I miss him."

She gives me a half smile. "Be patient. Hey, maybe we can do something this weekend."

"Just us?"

"Well, I mean Jared and I were planning on seeing a movie, but you can come with, and he can bring a friend."

I sneer. "Are you trying to set me up?"

"No. Not at all. I'm just saying it's an option, or maybe we can do something just you and me on Sunday. How about we have a sleepover? I'll pick you up after the movie and we hang out, make pancakes?"

It sounds great. It also sounds like a pity party just for me. I don't want a pity anything.

"Or not. I'm sorry, I'm a terrible friend right now. Jared and I are so new, and I have soccer, school, the end of the year project, and reading time at the library. What would you like me to do? Name it," Juliet says.

This is the part I hate. The guilt. I shouldn't try to mess up her new relationship because I'm so needy. If I'm honest with myself, I should really focus on my project. It's not going to get finished by itself.

"Hey, Adaline," one of the sophomores in Junior Elites says, interrupting my train of thought. I blink. I think her name is Hailey, but I can't remember.

"I was told to see you about the next fundraiser and what the prom theme was this year? You're in charge of that stuff, right? I'm class president of the sophomore class, and we're supposed to help decorate."

I nod. "Yeah. Um." Shit! How could I forget about prom? It's my only duty in Junior Elites; organize themes for the dances. "I still have to talk to Lacy Meyers about what they decided on."

"Okay, here's my number. Please call me with the details as soon as you get them. I have to get back to class."

Some boy walks by and the girl practically swoons into my lap. "You okay?" I ask.

She flushes and says, "What? Yeah. I uh. I gotta go. Call me with those details." She spins around and practically bolts from the lunch room.

Juliet laughs. "Aw, poor girl has it bad."

"Has what bad?" I ask.

She smiles. "Did you see the way Kayleigh looked at that boy? She's in love with him. That's how Chase used to look—" her eyes widen. "Crap. I'm sorry Addy. Ugh."

"It's fine. I guess I'm blind to the look. Her name is Kayleigh, not Hailey?"

"Yeah. She runs track. I think. I see her on the field when we're practicing and obviously at Junior Elites."

"So who's that clown?" I ask pointing to the boy she almost fainted over.

Juliet scrunches up her nose. "Um, I don't remember. Might be a football player."

"Who might be a football player?" Jared asks as he sets my Pepsi down and takes his seat next to Juliet.

She smiles. "That boy over there," she says to him.

"Tall guy with blond curls?" Jared asks.

"Yeah," I answer.

He smirks. "You interested, Addy? I can introduce you. His name is Maddock Fitch. Sophomore. He's going to be a kick-ass tight end next year. Well, I mean he's already a kick-ass tight end, but he'll be starting next year for sure."

I scowl. "I'm not looking for a boyfriend. One of the Junior Elites was checking him out."

Jared nods. "Cool. So did you ask Addy about the weekend after her birthday bash?"

"Ask me what about a week after?" I cock a brow in my friend's direction.

She blushes. "Not exactly," she says to him. She looks over at me. "Okay, so, there was this bowling thing happening, and since you like to bowl, I um, well, I kind of said you'd go with us."

I frown. "I don't want to go anywhere. I have this project to do. I also have to plan prom."

"You've been so depressed lately. And you said it yourself that this next project is making you lack inspiration. Come bowl. Get inspired. I promise it will help you work through your mojo."

"You mean to be the fifth wheel again. I'm good," I stand up, taking my things with me. "Count me out."

"It won't be like that, there is going to be about ten of us," she says.

I continue to walk away. There is nothing worse than your friend taking pity on your non-existent love life.

I'm almost out of the commons area when I run right into Chase. The look on his face sets my thoughts in overdrive. Yeah, I take back the pity. This is way worse.

Chapter Twenty

Adaline

C hase glares at me. "Adaline."

"I'm sorry. I'm so, so sorry."

He rolls his eyes. "So, I hear. Thank goodness you didn't take it out on my backside; I'm still recovering from the knife in my heart."

"Chase! Seriously, stop it." The look he gives practically kills me. "I can't keep doing this with you. I'm sorry you feel like this. I honestly am. I never meant for you to ever feel like that toward me."

"Well, I did. Now, I need to go to the drafting room." He starts to leave.

I grab his arm. "No. We need to talk about this."

He glares at my hand locked onto his arm then at me. He sighs. "Just let me go, Addy. I don't want to talk. There's nothing to say."

"There's plenty to say, Chase! You're just being a jackass." I let him go and storm away from him. I never asked my best friend to fall in love with me. I never gave him false hope to think we could be married and have kids. He did. Now, he looks at me like I crushed our entire imaginary future with one phrase.

I can't take it back. I won't. That would be cruel and undeserved. No matter how much I love and cherish our friendship. I will never let him think I love him more than I would a brother. I would never let him think there could be some future of us holding hands and kissing. There won't be.

So why do I feel like I'm the asshole here?

Chapter Twenty-One

Austin

Detention is like hell. Because I have to remain seated, quiet, and have absolutely no food in here. My stomach is growling like a mother-effer. The one person I'm happy to sit close to is also not looking at me at all. Yes, I'm in complete hell.

I can smell hints of Adaline's scent, and wow does she smell amazing. I clear my throat to get her attention, but she refuses to lift her gaze from her paper or acknowledge me in any way. It's like I'm dead to her.

I'm tempted to toss a ball of paper at her, but that's what got us into this silent treatment in the first place.

Mrs. Dinger opens a book and begins reading. It looks like some crap my mom reads. A guy with some long hair, some puffy pirate shirt all open in the middle with a little bit of his chest showing. Some chick in a dress with wind blowing in her hair standing next to him.

I want to tease Adaline and ask if she thinks it's a good

book because she's always reading something. Nothing with those kinds of covers, hers are more like balls of fire, or drops of water, or something like that.

Mrs. Dinger giggles at something then she looks up. "Don't you have homework to do, Mr. Reed?"

"I finished it at lunch. But I do have an end of the year project with Adaline. Do you mind if we discuss it?"

Adaline shoots a look at me. Her eyes aren't easy to read, so I'm not sure what she's thinking. Most of the time I can tell simple things like: this isn't a great idea, this is awesome, or she wants something.

"If you want to?" I add to Adaline.

She looks away from me and then back to Mrs. Dinger. "I don't care."

Mrs. Dinger nods. "Don't be loud or disruptive."

"Hey, does that mean I can talk?" Trent asks.

"No. You can sit there and do your homework," Mrs. Dinger says.

Trent throws his arms up and glares over at Adaline and me. "Great. It's like class all over again. The favorites and their privileges."

"Ignore him," I whisper to Ads.

She shifts in her seat and hands me over a notebook. "It's all there. I don't really need to talk to you either."

Well, shit.

Chapter Twenty-Two

Adaline

Why can't I stop thinking about him? I'm safely inside my house, away from his charming smile and sexy stares. He's a nuisance.

I pull out my cell and skim through my texts. I hit the call sign on one of the names, and it rings. Two to be exact before I hear the infamous, "Yo, it's Chase. Say it or text it."

I am about to hang up but the beep comes, and all of the sudden I'm charged. "You know what, I'm mad at you! You can be ticked off, but so can I. We were friends, and you just drop this huge bomb on me, expect me to deal, then you just quit being my friend. That's a douche move, Chase!"

My line beeps. "I hope you're happy!" I hang up on him and answer the other.

"Don't call me anymore, Adaline," Chase says.

"Don't tell me what to do," I snap at Chase.

He sighs. "You left a voicemail this time?"

"You don't respond."

"What do you want from me?"

I take a seat on my bed. "I want you to talk to me. I need my friend. I need you."

"I don't know if I can be that guy anymore."

I want to scream "Why?" But I know why. This hurts him. Maybe he did fall in love with me. Maybe I'm selfish because all I want is for him to have never asked me to the dance. I want us to go back to how things were. That's not being fair to him, though. Not really.

"Addy, my dad needs me. I gotta go." He hangs up without saying goodbye.

I remain there with the phone still pressed to my cheek and whisper, "Bye."

"Well, look who decided to grace us with her all-mightiness. Not all of us have no lives before or after school," Rachel snaps as I rush over to the lunch table where we all agreed to meet before the first bell.

I want to roll my eyes. I want to snap at Rachel. She's right, though. I'm fifteen minutes late. Juliet had soccer conditioning super early this morning, so getting my usual ride with her was not an option. I would have been on time if I had a license. I know this. Obviously, I don't, so this resulted in taking a bus, which was behind schedule.

Austin shoots a glare at Rachel. "Why don't you chill? She can be a little late."

"No. She's right. I shouldn't. It won't happen again. Um,

here's something Austin and I came up with while we were in detention." It's sort of a lie. I came up with it, and he looked it over.

Rachel snorts. "Are we being for real here? You made Zander and Lucas managers?" She chuckles as if it's funny. "On top of that, I already told you, Frost Queen—we're not building a skateboard ramp in the park. I mean, hello, does anyone else smell a lawsuit, or is it just me?" She shoves the plans away with a sneer.

"It's not ideal. We can place a bunch of safety features on it," I say. I was trying to find something that Zander and Lucas would actually participate in. They hang out with the skaters in school, so I thought this would work. Speaking of Lucas, I have no idea where he is. I do know one thing: this is turning into a major pain in my ass.

"So it can be lame?" Zander asks in a bored tone. "That's not cool. The danger is what makes it fun. 'No thrill. No reward.'"

Austin lowers his phone and says, "What the hell are you talking about? The phrase is 'No pain. No gain.'"

"I don't care what the stupid saying is. We're not doing this. Now, if you'll excuse me, I need to be somewhere else." Rachel pushes up from the table and saunters off.

I grab my notebook from the middle and place it back into my bookbag. Zander tilts his chair. "Dude, she's so strung out."

Austin looks at me then over at Zander. "Where's your partner in crime. I thought he was coming." Austin asks.

"Uh … right. He doesn't come to school until about eleven."

"Wait, how is he supposed to know what's going on if he's not here?" I ask.

Zander shrugs. "Call him. In fact, I think from now on you all should just text us. Here's my number." He slides me over a business card and winks.

I glance at it and then look over at Zander. "You have a picture of a weed leaf on your card."

Zander smiles. "Sure do. If you need some, hit me up. I even got some other stuff."

My eyes widen. "She's not hitting you up for anything," Austin says, plucking the card from my hand. "We'll keep in touch, though."

Austin's hand slides down my back, and he says, "Come on Ads. I'm walking you to class."

"I … um … " Yeah, I got nothing. I let myself enjoy the feel of his hand on my back while he walks me to first period.

I'm about halfway to first period when he says, "I can't believe Zander was hitting on you."

"Wh-what? No, he wasn't."

"Uh. Yeah. He was. That whole him trying to hook you up with weed was a ploy. He was hoping you'd call so he could ask you out."

"Don't be ridiculous."

Austin turns me, so I have to face him. "I'm not. Every straight guy in this school can see how sexy you are. I mean, hell, you've got three practically banging down your door."

I shake my head. "No, I don't."

He smiles. "Yeah, you do. It's so cute how blind you are to it. Fletcher, Bromwell, and me."

I roll my eyes and shift away from him. "Now I know you're full of crap."

Austin is beside me in an instant. "How do you figure?"

"Chase maybe but you and Greg? Please. You're just trying to butter me up so you can get a good grade."

"I don't need to butter you up, Adaline. Especially not if what I'm saying is true." We pause just outside my first-period class, and he stares at me for a moment. His dazzling eyes make my insides melt. He winks and leaves me with those words rattling through my head first thing this morning.

Damn, Austin Reed.

Chapter Twenty-Three

Austin

I love this girl. Yep. I said it. I love her.

Adaline stares me down at lunch. I smirk at her cute scowl. "What are you looking at?" Jared asks. He and Tyler are sitting at the table for the rest of the week.

"None of your business."

"Ha. If we would have said this to him, you know he would have been hounding us until we told him. Who is she?" Tyler asks.

I take a bite of my pizza and shrug. "Right. Well, I just hope to hell it's not Rachel," Tyler says.

I swallow. "It's not."

"Wow. Really?" Jared says.

I glare at him. "Yeah. We don't have shit in common."

Tyler smacks my arm. "You weren't singing that tune a few months ago. Who is it? Seriously, I need to thank this girl."

I push his arm off mine. "I'm not telling you fools

anything. It's not even like that." Because for one, the girl is still ticked at me. Two, I don't need a bunch of dumb rumors spreading around the school. Last, these knuckleheads will tell their girls, and then they'll try to get involved. Again, I don't need any of that. If I'm going to win Ads over, it has to be my way.

Jared gives me a look and smiles. "If you need someone to do a little digging for you, I can," he says.

"Aw, no fair. You know who it is, don't you?" Tyler says. "You're going to clue me in on it later."

Jared shakes his head. "I don't know. I have an idea. I don't think I should clue you in, though. Austin looks like he's about to blow his top over there. Like when we make mom jokes at him."

He's right. I do not like them making mom jokes at me. I also don't want them to get any ideas about hooking me up with the person they think I'm talking about. It would put me in the doghouse with Adaline if they ended up being wrong.

Adaline gets up from her table and marches over to mine. She slaps a notebook beside my tray, and I look up at her. "Hey, Ads. What brings you around?"

"Since you have detention, here is this to look over." She darts a look from me to Tyler then Jared, then returns back to me. "Uh, because you know Rachel thought our idea was terrible."

I roll my eyes at the mention of that fiasco this morning. To be fair, Rachel does have a good point, at the same time I have no idea what other things we could do to keep Zander and Lucas around. We need those yo-yos in order to get a good grade. That's the shit part about this group project—if we all don't participate, all of our grades drop. Did I mention we had to have video proof?

If we could have done this shit without the video proof, we could have totally cut those jackholes right out.

"So when do you think you can work on the project? Rachel said she's available after school, but, and I quote, 'If I screw with her Friday and Saturday nights, she will murder me in the parking lot and make it look like an accident.' I know you have to work."

I run my hand through my hair. "Right, about that. I actually um, have to find a new job. So for now, except for today and tomorrow, you have me whenever you want."

She blushes. "Uh. Okay." She tucks a piece of her blond hair behind her ear. "Good chat."

As soon as she walks away, Tyler says, "I'm curious. How's working with Frost again? Usually, you're hiding from her, but you two looked pretty chummy from here."

"We're kosher, that's all. What?" I ask Jared when I spot his cocky grin.

"Nothing. Not a thing," Jared says.

Tyler is now laughing, and I decide to mull over the notebook while eating the rest of my lunch. Jackasses. My friends are a bunch of jackasses. Wonder if they figured out Adaline is the one I want to make my girlfriend?

Chapter Twenty-Four

Adaline

I try to be accommodating. I really do, but wow, sometimes I just want to choke the life out of this group of idiots I'm paired up with. Rachel decides at the last minute that the time I have down is not good enough for her. She has a nail appointment and that, my friends, changes for no one. Lucas, well, he doesn't even bother coming to school. Zander was right beside me, and now I have no idea where the hell he went.

Austin strolls into Bradfield Park where we all agreed to meet and says, "Am I early?"

"Nope. Zander disappeared, and everyone else was a no-show." I pull out my phone and show him the text from Rachel.

"Ads, I'm sorry. I know how much grades mean to you. Don't worry, I'll get them all here one way or another."

I nod. Honestly, I feel like crying. This is why I usually do this on my own or with people I trust. Principal Briggs is probably in his office laughing it up about his randomly picked groups. I should have taken my aunt's offer and moved to France for this semester. My mom wanted me to have more culture; it is supposedly good for your soul.

Yes, I could be sitting in a little café, eating divine pastries with my cousin, Sophie. Instead, I'm here losing my mind. Why did I say no? I wouldn't be in this situation right this second.

"Addy, did you hear me?" Austin asks.

"Yeah," I swipe a stray tear and say, "you are going to fix this somehow."

"Right, that was earlier. I said this is a great compromise you came up with. I think we can pull it off."

I blink at him. "Oh, uh, yeah. I was just throwing ideas out there. So you think building a boardwalk would be better?"

"Yeah. I do. This way people can ride bikes or skateboard, and we won't have to tear it down. Which park? And where should we put it? We'll need Rachel to get her dad to approve it ASAP."

"Right." Another reason I needed her here today, but of course, she couldn't bother.

Austin looks left then right. "I think over there is the best spot if you want to do it here." He points to a corner of the park that's shaded but has enough open space to build our project.

"The idea was to place it here because it's in the center of town, also closest to our school."

Austin smiles. "I like your thinking, Frost. Come on, let's make sure that ground over there is stable."

"Why wouldn't it be?"

"Have you seen some parks after a good rain? Some need new draining in sections. Let's hope this is not the case here. Otherwise, this could be way more work than we want to get into."

I curl my lip. I was not in the mood for any more work, especially if only two of us showed up. We might as well slap a big F on this thing right now. And if I get an F, what will that mean for my future? I won't be taking those college classes like my parents want me to, that's for sure. I can't bear to see my parents looking at me like I'm a failure.

Austin nudges me as we walk toward the spot where we plan on building. "You have that glum expression again. Everything is going to be okay. I promise."

I stop walking and stare at him. "How can you say something like that? You can't promise this will be fixed. You know as well as I do this is a disaster."

Austin turns and continues walking backward. "Adaline Bea Frost, the girl with the most interesting name ever. I promise I won't let you down. Not again. Now, quit scowling at me and get over here."

He calls my name interesting, and for the first time ever I find myself liking my name. Strange. Argh. What am I saying? This is a no. This is how he pulls me in, and then I'll be pining after him again.

I reluctantly walk over to where he is but refuse to look at him.

"Well, the ground seems solid. No soft spots. Go check that side." He directs me near a set of trees to the left of us.

I don't see any mud puddles, but according to him, that

means diddly squat. I walk the path, and my shoe is instantly soggy. I pull out my tennis shoe and make a face. Mushy mud cakes it. I say, "Gawh! This is gross!"

Austin snickers. "Did you find a spot?" He runs over still chuckling. "Oh, yeah. Didn't you see the grass is two different shades?"

"I don't find this funny." I'm about to shake off the mud from my sneaker on him like a dog shakes out its wet fur. Bet he'd stop laughing then.

As I imagine him squirming and getting all ticked 'cause mud landed on his face, shirt, and jeans a giggle pops out of my mouth. Then I suddenly squeal as he scoops me up and pulls me away from the squishy ground.

"What are you doing? Put me down!" I demand.

Austin is still laughing. "It's fine. Hold still, or you might have your ass covered in mud too. I don't want to drop you."

"I can walk, Austin." His face is so close to mine. I don't like this position; I also don't hate it either. From here I can easily kiss him. I can count every stray freckle. I can see the stubble growing along his jawline. And don't get me started on his scent. Man, why does he have to smell so good? Like rainwater and lemons.

He smiles. "You okay there? I don't want you to fall asleep on me."

"I didn't fall asleep."

"Your eyes were closed." He sets me down on a bench far from the spot where we were. "Give me your shoe."

"No." I remember this trick when we were kids. He stole my shoe and threw it up in a tree. I had to climb it to get it back down. I'm not doing that again.

He shakes his head. "So stubborn." He yanks my sneaker off my foot.

"Hey! You better put that back on my foot, Austin, or I'll find a stick to beat you with."

He looks back at me with an amused expression. "Testy. I'll be right back. Just stay put. Please."

I hobble off the bench. "You come back with my footwear."

"For the love of it, will you go sit your ass down? I will bring back your precious shoe in a second. Trust, just a little is all I'm asking here, Ads. Now, go sit down. We all know how you are in one-legged races."

I flush at his words and hop back to the bench. I plop down with my arms folded and sneer at his backside. Austin was a dirty cheat in that race when we were kids. He tripped me right before I hit the finish line.

A few minutes later, Austin returns with a white and pink sneaker free of any mud. He kneels in front of me and says, "All right, Cinderella, let's get you your slipper."

I slide my foot into my shoe, and he laces it up and ties it. I'm gushing at this silly moment. At the same time, I want to put my wall up and yell at him that I'm not five and can tie my own darn shoes. I don't want to fall for him again, but it's becoming more and more difficult when he keeps doing stuff like this. I need a new strategy.

"I uh … gotta go," I say as he gently releases my foot.

He gives me a puzzled look and says, "How are you getting home?"

"Bus."

"The hell you are. Come on."

I shake my head. "I can take the bus."

He stands up and extends his hand out to me. "You aren't taking a bus."

"I really—"

"I said no." He leans in and takes my hand then pulls me, so I'm next to him. "Get a move on, or I'll carry you. Either way, I'm not letting you ride a bus."

Did I ever mention he's the most persistent person I've ever encountered, and sometimes it can be really annoying? Like now. He's getting on my nerves. Why can't he just let me be? Doesn't he know I need this space to clear my head and my heart? There's gotta be some way out of working with him. Has to be. Otherwise, my heart is in total trouble.

Chapter Twenty-Five

Austin

Adaline is so set in her ways. Sometimes it drives me crazy. Sue me—I don't want the girl I like a lot to ride a freaking bus. I know what types of people are on the bus. They live in my section of town. Those people don't need to be anywhere near someone as sweet and innocent as Adaline.

As I close the passenger door, I walk over to the driver's side and pause when my cell rings. I slip it out of my jeans and hit answer on the unknown caller. "Hello?"

"I'm looking for an Austin Reed."

If this is a bill collector, so help me, I'm not in the mood. "Yes." I walk away from my car in case that's what this happens to be. I can't have Adaline overhearing me.

"Joe called me. Told me you were the hardest working kid he's had at the shop. Said you needed some work. Are you interested?"

"Uh, sure. Who is this again?"

The guy laughs. "Sorry, I've been so busy around here

I thought I said my name. I'm Harvey. I have a shop just outside of Riverside. Are you able to come in today?"

"Yeah. You fixed my friend Jared's truck?" I start to return to my car with a smile.

"I did. You know my shop then, that's good. What time can I expect you?"

I throw a fist in the air and smile. "I can get there in thirty minutes." Finally, my luck is starting to change.

"All right." We hang up, and I slide into my car.

"Was that good news or something?" Adaline says from the passenger seat.

I shrug. "It was good. Why?"

"You've been looking stressed out lately," she says as she looks away from me.

Stressed? Of course, I am. "I'm fine."

I catch the slight lift of her shoulders from the corner of my eyes. "You're such a liar."

"I'm not stressed."

"Bull. Anyone with your life would be stressed out. Austin, it's me. I know what you are going through."

I know she's trying to help, but her words tick me off. "You know what I'm going through, do you? Tell me something, Adaline, have you ever had to worry about if this is the day someone will evict you? Have you ever had to worry about having hot water in the morning? Or even heat during the winter?" She doesn't say a word, so I continue. "That's what I thought. Face it, Ads, you live in a palace. You don't have shit to worry about. I have to deal with this crap on the daily, and my home is far from luxury. So never, ever, tell me you know anything of what I'm going through."

"I only meant—"

"I know what you meant. Everyone says the same shit to me. Just be lucky it's not how you live."

I glance over at her in time for her to dart her eyes out the side window. "I'm sorry. I won't ask again," she mumbles.

My shoulders slump. Way to wreck any progress you made with the girl. I keep driving to her house in silence.

She hops out of my vehicle as if the thing is on fire. I don't bother getting out because she's almost at her front door. I do wait until she enters her house. After that, I hightail it out of there. No use sitting around waiting.

I drive to the garage where I am now going to be working. Joe's garage wasn't the nicest joint. Some of the windows were different colors. Not on purpose. I think he was just fixing it cheap. There were a few times I was worried a skinny kid like me would become someone's lunch. So I'm happy that this new place is on the better side of town.

The garage I pull up to is packed, hardly any parking left in the lot. The other thing I notice is how nice the outside of the shop looks.

I step out with my coveralls and boots in my hand and walk in through the main door. What I assume are customers in business attire and way better clothes than me look over at me. One lady sneers as if I was gum on the bottom of her fancy heels. Great. Country club types come here.

A girl behind the desk whips away from me with a yellow

slip in her hand and says, "Just a second."

"No problem."

Her red hair swishes from one side to the other as she spins in her chair to a sliding glass window. She jostles it open and shouts, "Yo. Harv. Your newbie is here."

She slams the window shut then looks back at me. "He'll be with you."

As I stand there waiting, she works away on her computer or whatever. She looks a little older, like she may have already graduated from college, or is attending it. Not sure. Somewhere in there, though. I definitely wouldn't peg her for a high school student because she's got a small sign of crow's feet at the edges of her eyes.

"Hey, you must be Austin." A fairly tall man says in a gruff voice. He wipes his hands on the rag then sticks one out at me. I grab and shake like I should.

"Come with me," he says. He leads me to a door past the customers and off to the side. I assume we are going to his office, but he redirects me to a break room of some sort. "I'm Harvey, where do you go to school at? You look a little young."

"Riverside High."

He takes a seat at a table and motions for me to do the same. "My nieces go there."

"Yeah, what're their names?"

"Valentine. Juliet and Layla."

I almost topple out of my chair. "Wait a second. Juliet and Layla Valentine, yeah, I know them."

He laughs. "Joe and I have been friends for a long time. Anyway, he said business has been a little slow lately, and he didn't have any work for you. But you were a great worker and since I'm in need of some more hands to give you a call."

I run my hands through my hair. "Joe is really great."

"So, are you okay with working from 5:00 to close. We close up around 8:00 Monday through Friday and at 9:00 on Saturday. We don't work Sundays because that's the Lord's day. Does this sound like a schedule that fits yours?"

It does, but also it doesn't. I'm not going to be able to help with the class project Monday to Friday, and Adaline is gung-ho set on her schedule. But my mom and I need the income. "It'll work. I'll be here," I say.

Harvey stands up and shakes my hand. Great. Let's get the paperwork started.

Chapter Twenty-Six

Adaline

The weekend feels like a blessing and a nightmare all rolled in one. I can sleep in past seven, so it's a blessing. My mom gets to harp on me about my college choices, so it's a nightmare. I just don't want to deal with it today.

"Adaline, we need to have a discussion about this. We've got to figure out your options now, so you can focus on the things you need to do to get there. Instead of going about it blindly like everyone else does. If we wait until you're a senior, it's too late. And technically, you are taking senior courses now," my mom says as she waves her top college choices in my face as I enter the kitchen heading to the coffee pot.

I want to groan at her and tell her coffee first, everything else second. But she's not letting up. "Are you going to talk to me about this?"

I give her side-eyes. "I just woke up. Give me a minute."

"Fine. I suppose your future has a minute."

I swear she acts like my future is on a time-bomb, like

if I don't have a decision right this second, it will blow up. I pour coffee into a cup and start drinking as I walk around my mom. She's following me into each room I enter. I take a seat on the couch and flick on the TV.

"Really? Adaline, I'm trying to talk about your life, and you want to watch reality TV?"

I set my mug down and turn to her. "Mom, I love you, but you need to back off. It's too much."

She frowns. "I want what's best for you. That Reed boy, I fear, is a distraction for you."

"Austin is not even an issue. We just have to do a project together." It's not a total lie. Austin made it clear he doesn't want me involved in his life. So I'm not. "Since the first day of my junior year you've been on my case about choosing a college." I just don't want to think about it. I don't want to make this so final.

My mom sets down her college books and sighs. "You're right. I guess I've been a little harsh on you." I give her the "ya think" look. "Okay. Way harsh. I just know how these things go. Your cousin is a prime example. She waited until the last minute to decide where she wanted to go and got waitlisted. I don't want that to be your same mistake."

I pat her leg and smile. "I promise I will let you know where I want to visit before spring break."

"Okay. Can you do me a favor, though? Can you at least look? Show me you are doing your research."

I nod and go back to enjoying my coffee. As soon as she leaves the room I push the book aside. My phone rings, jolting me, scaring the crap out of me. I answer it without checking the screen. "Hello?"

"Oh, you're up. Great. Want to hang out today? I feel like we hardly see each other," Juliet says.

"Hi. Yeah. Okay. I'm currently slumming it in my PJs," I say as I glance down at my comfy sweats.

"That's cool. I'm in bum mode too. Wanna hang out at my place or the book café?"

"Ooooh, good question. Hmmm. Will you still be in bum mode if we go to the book café? I'll be honest, I don't feel like changing out of this plush of comf yet."

She laughs. "Totally. We can rock the just-waking-up look. Although to be fair, I had a game this morning, so this is actually my relax gear."

"Sorry I missed it. How did you all do?"

"We won. I scored a few times."

"Why do you sound so depressed?" I ask.

"It's nothing. I'll be at your house in ten. Cool?"

"Yep."

We hang up, and I can't help thinking my friend is keeping something from me.

"Want to stop at the mall before we go to the book café?" Juliet asks as we drive farther from my house.

"Um, no. I look like I came straight out of a twister."

She looks over at me and smiles. "Me too. Who cares though, right? I gotta get something for ... " she fake coughs, "tonight."

I roll my eyes. "What's with the cough-tonight crap?

What are you trying to do, Juliet?"

"I want to say. I really do, but I can't."

"Why?"

She turns the wheel of her Wrangler and into the entrance of the mall. Once she finds a parking spot, she hops out. I reluctantly do the same. We enter one of the side doors leading us down a mostly deserted hallway aside from some stray candy machines which probably has ten-year-old candy inside them. Gross.

Juliet heads directly into Express. I raise a brow. "Um, so why are we in here? You never wore anything from here before. Oh, did Layla con you into getting her a top for her again?" That would make sense.

"No. I ... uh ... there's this party tonight, and I don't know. I want to look hot or hotter for Jared. Most of the in crowd wears this kind of stuff, so I figured it was the best place to start."

I glare at Juliet. "Please tell me this is not a repeat Mark thing. I will punch Jared right in his nose if it is."

"What? No. I'm doing this because I want to. Not because he said or did anything. He loves my wardrobe."

I study her a little more then nod. "All right." Mark, her ex-boyfriend, the douchewad who turned Austin against me when we were kids. He told her she should start dressing sexier so his friends wouldn't rag on him. So, Juliet started wearing makeup, not a lot, like blush and lip gloss and mascara. Before Mark, she wouldn't touch things like blush and mascara. Hell, the girl barely plucked her eyebrows. I had to do that for her, otherwise she might be walking around with two caterpillars stuck on her face.

I like Jared. He's good for Juliet. He always makes sure she's happy, and I for one am glad of that. I'm worried she's trying to change, when he likes her for who she is now. I think the vultures at our school may be getting to her. The ones who are waiting for her and Jared to break up, so they can swoop in and date him.

I pick up a pink lacey top and say, "What about this?"

She sticks her tongue out. "You know I don't like pink. That's something Layla would wear." Exactly.

I find the same top in black and cream. "How about these, then?"

"I like the black one. What do you think, though? Should I get something different?"

"Considering this is way different than you normally wear, I think you should probably keep one thing the same."

She nods. "Good thinking. What size do you have?"

"Small."

She grabs it from me and walks toward the changing rooms. "I'll be back."

I pretend to look through the clothes on the rack where I'm standing. A woman with a short, blond bob says, "Is there something you're looking for that I can help you find?"

"Oh, no. I'm just looking while waiting on my friend."

"Okay. If you change your mind, my name is Cam."

"Cool." She walks away, and I move on to another rack. I'm so bored.

Juliet finally comes out. The lacy top is nowhere in sight and tears flood her face. "What's wrong?" I ask.

"Nothing. Let's get out of here." She jerks me out of the store and down to the bookstore.

I pull back when we get past the Horror section. "What is wrong? Tell me."

She shakes her head. "I know you'll go ballistic. It's stupid. Really. I don't even know why I'm crying. I'll just borrow something from Layla."

I narrow my eyes. "Who was in the changing room?"

"What? No ... I'm not sure. It sounded like Kimber and Selena. They were um ... It doesn't matter. It's stupid."

"Bull. If it is so stupid, you wouldn't be upset. Those jerks said something about you, didn't they?"

Juliet walks toward the Teen section. "It doesn't matter. People think and say what they want. I shouldn't let them get to me like that."

"Juls, for the love of it. You need to put those witches in their place. Especially Kimber. Aren't you co-captain?"

Juliet's tears start up again. "What?" I ask.

"God, the way she dogged me in the changing room, it was awful. She said the only reason I got to be co-captain is because Lacy and I take turns sucking off Coach Harper."

"Are you shitting me? You can't let her go around saying things like that. Seriously, it's uncalled for, and you can get a crap ton of people in trouble with that rumor flying around."

"I know, but it's not like they knew I was there. I mean, I didn't see them when I was being checked into a room. They were already talking when the girl asked for my name."

I grab hold of my friend's arm and yank her out of the bookstore.

"What are you doing? Addy. Stop. Stop. We're not going back there."

I turn to my friend. "Yeah we are, and we're going to

knock the snot out of them."

"Addy. No. I'll handle it. I swear I will. I'll talk to Lacy and the coach and tell them I overheard some girls say some things. And if it starts going around school, it'll already be handled. Damage under control."

I crack my knuckles. "All right. I don't agree all the way but okay."

"Let's go to the café. This place is starting to get to me."

I nod. "You and me both."

We look at each other and laugh as we head to the exit that leads to the section of the parking lot where her Wrangler is.

Chapter Twenty-Seven

Austin

The last place I probably needed to be is at Tyler's party. It's Saturday, and I got off work, so here I am. Well, I've been here for an hour and a half. Same people doing the same crap, it's almost a bore.

I'm about to leave when Jared, Juliet, Adaline, and Greg walk through the door. The drink that was in my hand slips and drops to the white rug under my feet. Damn. It absorbs my rum and coke right up, leaving a huge brown stain. I sweep my foot across it a few times while I stare at Adaline walking toward the kitchen with Greg.

Her hands are at her side, but he has a hand on her lower back. I ditch my spot on the sofa and head into the kitchen. Greg is a few bodies in front of me. I could easily push one of these bystanders right into him, and hopefully he'd knock into a wall or something.

I'm just about to snatch him up by the back of the neck, but someone grabs me by my shoulder. They wheel me away from Greg. I glance over, and Tyler smirks. "I don't know exactly what you were about to do there, buddy, but I had to stop you. Come on. Beer pong time for you."

"I don't wanna play, man."

"Yeah, you do. You dominate at beer pong." He guides me over to a table set up in what we call his game room. "I figured out who you've been trying to score with too. Little advice, don't. She's not like Rachel."

I scowl at him. "Oh, well, thanks, Dad. Any other tips you got for me?"

"Nah, well, maybe two: don't call me Dad, and we better win. I don't want to be shitfaced before the night is over. Layla will kick my ass."

I shake my head and step up to the one end of the table. Tyler announces, "All right. My boy Austin and I are up. Who is playing against us?"

Layla suddenly appears by his side. "Tyler, I thought we agreed you'd behave," she says.

"Babe. Don't worry. Austin and I got this. Don't we?" He looks over at me, and I want to walk away. I want to hunt down Greg and rip his hands off his body so he can't place them on Adaline ever again.

"Bro, you got that look on your face again. I'm telling you, you better stay put. Play and get your mind focused on something else," Tyler says.

I sigh and look down at the other end of the table. Trent and Chris are there waiting for us to serve first. I'm no longer thinking about Greg but kicking Trent's ass in this game. With some hope, this ping-pong will get lodged in his throat.

I smirk at Tyler. "Give me the ball."

"Uh. Okay."

As soon as the smooth white ball rolls against my palm, my adrenaline increases. Just like it does before a football or basketball game. I got this.

I release the ball, and it flies right into the cup. Trent scowls. "Lucky shot, asshole."

"Luck had nothing to do with it. Those are skills," I say.

Tyler laughs then fist bumps me.

Trent and Chris are looking salty, but I don't give a damn. I sink four more shots. I'm about to go for number five. My attention is pulled from the cups as I spot Adaline weaving through the crowd that has formed around the beer pong game. My concentration slips, and I over toss, and the ball sails into the crowd. Tyler slaps my side. "It's cool, man. It's only one."

He shrugs and downs a cup. I tip back a cup myself. I'm not a big fan of shitty beer. During these games, Tyler always pours shit beer in the cups in case someone acts like an ass and knocks a cup off the table, or even the whole table. It happens, but it's not a complete waste.

I wince as the bitter liquid hits my tongue, and then I swallow. "Ugggg."

"Yeah, this is total balls," Tyler says as he winces.

"This has to be the reject version of beer. I don't think I have taste buds anymore."

Tyler nods. "I know. Wow. Shit. I need a chaser." Layla hands him over a Summer Shandy with a smile.

"You want me to get you one, Austin?" she asks.

I shake my head. "Nah. I can't get too lit. I still gotta get home." I also want to be able to have a conversation with Adaline and remember it.

Adaline is closer to the table now, Greg is there too. I hate this. Why is she with him? He can't have anything in common with her. Well, okay, maybe he's in advanced classes like her, but after that what other things are left? Nothing.

As I watch Greg gawk around the room as if he is looking for someone, I feel a slight sting against my arm. Dumbly I glance at the spot on my arm and then at the white ball doing a lap in the red Solo cup mere inches from me. "Shit."

"That doesn't count. The ball is out. It hit his arm," Tyler protests.

Chris sways. "Oh, it counts. It's called backboard."

"This isn't basketball, douche. We're not taking a cup away," Tyler says.

"You're such a cheat. Suck it up and drink," Trent presses.

I pull the ball from the cup and say, "Screw it. Let 'em have it."

"Nah man. That's straight bull. Put that cup down." Tyler stares down Trent and Chris and says, "It's a rule. I can't help it if you don't like it. You can walk your merry ass out the door."

Someone in the room says, "Oooooh," and a group forms.

Trent leans forward as if he's about to cause a bunch of trouble. I'm teetering on the edge, ready to pounce if necessary. Chris, though, leans back and says, "Whatever man. You wanna cheat? That's fine."

Tyler shrugs. "Think what you want. The rules are online. Look them up. But next time I'll print them out and post them for you. Since clearly, you don't know them."

Trent's temper flares. He tips the table and charges after Tyler like a bull. I'm not in the mood for this shit, though. I stick my arm out and clothesline Trent right at the chest.

Causing him to land flat on his back. He looks up at me stunned.

"There's no one here to pull me off of you this time, Trent. Stay down if you know what's good for you," I say.

He moves as if he's going to push himself up and come at me. I'm about to welcome it until I hear her gasp out, "Stop it."

I turn to Ads. Her eyes are wide and filling with tears. "Stop, Austin." Her silk-like fingers touch my arm, and she pulls. I drop my fist and swallow. I never want Adaline to see me like this. Here I am, scaring her. What's odd, I'm usually laid-back and not flying off the handle like this.

"Hey, none of that," I whisper to her as I swipe my thumb against her cheek.

Adaline blinks and then steps back. A body knocks into my side and hands crawl up my chest. "Wow. That was so hot," some brunette girl says.

I glance over at Adaline who is creating more distance between us. Damn it. Not again. I am about to shout at her, but Greg drapes his arm over her shoulder reminding me that I've already lost her. I hate reality.

The brunette grips my muscles, something that normally turns me on. Usually, I'd say something stupid like, "You like that? I'll gladly give you the whole tour of all my muscles." I have no interest in taking this girl anywhere, though. Her touch is annoying me.

I pry her fingers off my arm and smile. "I gotta get a drink. Mine ended up on the floor."

She bats her lashes. "I'll come with you. I'm Daisy. I've been dying to talk to you for three months."

"Uh. Why?" I ask not meaning to sound like a total ass. She doesn't seem to find me offensive, though. She continues to follow me out of the game room and into the kitchen.

She bumps into my arm and says, "Well, you're so hot and great at basketball."

"Thanks. You're a big basketball fan then?"

"The biggest."

I smile. "Yeah. Who's your favorite team? Mine's the Lake."

"Oh, I'm a huge Lake fan."

Someone in the room laughs. I hate fake girls. Just because I like and play basketball doesn't mean everyone else does. So I don't expect them to. Same with football.

I hear Juliet from the corner. "It's the Lakers. Not the Lake."

"The what?" Daisy asks.

"Austin was messing with you. The Lake isn't even a real team," Jared says as he passes a cup to his girlfriend.

I shrug. "Sorry. I don't like when people fake things."

Daisy scowls, rolls her eyes, and stomps off to the living room, which everyone seems to have turned into a dance floor. I pour myself a coke and look over at Jared who's laughing. "Wow. You really know how to piss a girl off," he says.

"That's not my fault. How long has Fletcher and Ads been dating?" I ask Juliet.

She chokes on her drink and starts coughing. "They aren't," Jared answers for her as he rubs her back.

"You sure about that?" I ask.

They both nod. I gotta make a move then before that asshat swoops in and takes her for good. I grab my drink and set off toward the crowded dance room.

Chapter Twenty-Eight

Adaline

I have no idea why I stopped Austin from hitting Trent in the face. Now, it's all I seem to think about. I've been home for nearly two hours since Greg and I left Tyler's party. The smarter more sensible version of myself would have spent that time thinking about the project. I'm losing it.

I punch my pillow again and scream. "Aghhhhh!" I should go to sleep. I should not think about Austin or that look he gave me as I gripped his arm and told him to stop.

I flip around and shut my eyes, trying to drown out the entire night. I give up again after a few minutes. I shoot out of bed and begin pacing my room like a crazy person in my unicorn PJs.

A tap outside my room causes me to still and turn to my French doors. Austin is there with a baseball cap on and dressed in dark clothing aside from his varsity jacket which has some strips of orange threaded through the black. I shouldn't let him in. My head is screaming at me not to.

Apparently, I have crappy listening skills and open the door. "What are you doing here?"

He turns his cap backward while approaching me like a cat stalking its prey. Then his lips crash against mine, and I'm consumed by all these feelings. First, there is the bubbling sensation starting in my heart, swarming to my stomach, and then shooting throughout my body from my toes to my head. Then the feel of his tongue swiping across mine. His minty breath coats my lips, mouth, and wow I can't get enough. His fingers entwine through my hair and run down my spine.

He gently breaks our kiss and presses his forehead to mine. "I needed to give you that."

I stare at his lips. "Why?"

"Because you left without me wishing you goodnight and telling you thank you."

I pull back to study his eyes.

No. Dang it, Adaline, this is what gets your heart broken. Do not fall for his charms or his kisses. Even if he kisses as if it's the last time he's ever going to see you, making it so darn perfect all you do is stupidly swoon.

Again. Crappy listener. I smile at him as heat blossoms across my cheeks. "Well, you could have texted it," I say.

Austin smirks. "I could, but wasn't that better?"

I remain silent.

Austin stops touching me and steps away. I don't want him to walk away. I want him back to where he was. At least I think I do. I shake my head and sigh. "You should probably get home. My parents will be up soon."

"Yeah. Get some sleep. I'll call you at noon, so we can work on the design." He makes his way to the doors. He pauses by the balcony. "Oh, and Ads?"

"What?"

"I like the PJs." He winks at me then climbs the tree like a monkey. I'm so screwed.

Okay, I thought Austin visiting me last night was somehow a dream. Until he says, "Aw no unicorn PJs? I was kind of hoping you'd still have them on."

My eyes bulge. "You need to quit visiting my room."

"Is that going to be a rule?"

I fold my arms. "It can be."

He rolls his eyes. "Whatever. Let's go over this stuff, so you can get back to your plans with ding-ding Fletcher."

I scowl at him. "I don't have plans with Greg, and he's not a ding-ding. You probably have plans with chesty the brunette."

"The who? Oh, the freshman all over me last night? Are you jealous?"

"Why would I be jealous? You can date who you want. You apparently have a type: big boobs, no brains. How original." Although he is right, I'm jealous but also mad. I mean, how could he even kiss me and flirt with whoever comes along. It drives me nuts.

He throws down his notebook on the table in the library and snaps. "That's what I want, is it? Wow, you know me so freaking well, Frost. Bet you're giving yourself a ton of gold stars for that guess."

I pick up my things from the table and scoot my chair out. "I think I should get home."

"I just got here."

"Well, you were late, and as you so elegantly put it, I have other plans."

Austin plops down in the chair, dips his head, and runs his fingers through his hair. "I'm never going to win with you am I, Adaline?"

"What do you mean?" I ask as I slip one of the straps of my bag over my shoulder.

His eyes lock with mine. "I'm always screwing up. Not agreeing to go to the dance with you. Kissing you last night when you probably wish it was someone else. Now, showing up late. I'm sorry. I just … I won't try anymore."

I reluctantly slump back down in my chair. "From now on don't kiss me anymore, and don't be late. Okay?"

"Fine."

I pull my things back out of my bag. "I've been thinking about this, and I think we should not only build the boardwalk, but what if we added book chambers? We can call it a reading lane."

"Book what?" he asks.

I flip through the pages of my notebook. Forcing myself not to look into his eyes so I can remain focused. "You know the park with the secret reading compartments? Juliet and I always take books there for kids to take and read."

"So, you want to make a project on giving away books?" Austin asks.

I narrow my eyes at him because I heard the tone in his voice. He thinks I'm going to be a typical geek and come up with some nerdy idea. "I think it would be good. Don't you? It will hit two requirements on our list: educational and contributing to the community."

Austin rubs his jawline. "It sounds great and easy to make, but I have a feeling dirty minds might get involved and try to sneak in overly entertaining things into the mix. Obviously, we wouldn't want a five-year-old coming home with some erotica or a random dirty magazine."

"That's why we'd monitor the boxes daily and make them at different heights. So every box would be age appropriate."

He nods. "I get it. I like this idea a lot. All right, let's write down all the materials we'll need."

Austin and I get to work listing out things we'd need. The one big thing we'd need is the stocked entertainment. "I can go to the comic store that Juliet and I stop at in the mall. I'll ask if they'd like to donate to our box," I say.

"I can probably hit up libraries and second-hand shops."

"What can we assign Rachel, Zander, and Lucas to do?" I ask.

"We're going to need snacks and stuff. Although, I'm afraid of what they might come back with," he says, making a face.

I laugh. I'm a little nervous too. "Maybe we should make them get the supplies?" But even that sounds risky in my head. See, those three were supposed to be at this meeting too. Rachel canceled at the last second saying she had an important dinner party with her dad. I remember overhearing Layla telling Juliet to cut Rachel some slack because her life isn't all jewels and glam. Apparently, it's a lot of spotlights and keeping up appearances. Maybe this is why Rachel is the way she is, who knows. I certainly don't.

Zander and Lucas didn't bother telling me anything. Honestly, they're probably still in bed. Sleeping off a hangover or something. I saw them yesterday at Tyler's party, and let's just say they didn't even know my name let alone their own.

I gnaw on the idea a little more. "You know what? Maybe we should just get the supplies."

Austin drops his pencil and leans back in his seat. "We could, but this is supposed to be a group effort. We're supposed to videotape us taking and tackling certain tasks. We're also supposed to be working as a group in the end. We can't just come up with an idea, get the supplies, the donations, and build this all without them. We'll get an F just as easy if we aren't all participating. You heard Mrs. Martin."

"I know. It is a little difficult to get anything done, though, if no one shows up except you and me. And some of us are not on time." I look up at him.

He frowns. "Yeah I know I was late. I had to do something for work."

"I thought you told me you didn't have a job anymore."

"I got one recently. Don't give me the look, Ads. I need the money more than I need this grade. It's bullshit that the school puts so much pressure on us to finish this project or face failure." I can see the frustration in his eyes. He rakes his fingers through his hair. "Lately, I've been on the losing end of things. I'm days away from possibly getting evicted because we're behind. This project is turning out to be more of a failure than a success. Then there is ... never mind." He shoots his chair out and loads up his things into his backpack.

"Where are you going?"

"Back to work. Don't worry I'll get things on my end taken care of. You just … take care of your list."

Just like that, he disappears. I shouldn't care, but I do. He opened up and shut me out so fast my head is still spinning. This is why I need to stay away from Austin Reed.

Chapter Twenty-Nine

Austin

I swear I keep digging myself deeper into a hole instead of getting out of it. I made some headway with Adaline and then effed it all up like usual.

I told her I had to work, but that's a lie. It's Sunday, and the shop is closed. I slip inside my house and head toward my room. My mom is sitting at the kitchen table with a stack of bills and a calculator.

"How is the project coming along?" she asks without looking up at me.

"It's not." I redirect my steps and enter the kitchen instead.

I place a hand over my mom's, and she pauses at punching more digits into the calculator. Her eyes meet mine, and I smile. "You know you don't have to worry about this much longer. I should have enough to cover all this plus this month's."

She looks away. "Honey, I don't want you to spend most

of your school year in the shop. We moved here because it's cheaper. Plus, if I work enough shifts at the diner, I'll be able to cover everything, and we'll still have some left over."

"But Mom, you hate that place. You hate this place. We don't belong here. We belong in our house." I take a seat next to her. "Don't you want it back?"

She sighs. "There aren't many good memories there. We were constantly struggling. I was unhappy. This isn't where I want to spend the rest of my life, but it's okay for now."

I can't believe she's saying this. It's like she's given up completely, and I feel like it's my fault. She wouldn't say any of this if we were still in our house and had our crap together. I get up from the table and make my way to the fridge. I open it, and it's bare. Cupboards are the same.

"We need to go to the store, I know," she says from the table. "I wanted to see what I could spend without cleaning us out until my next paycheck."

Broke and starving, yeah, I hate this. This life really sucks. I put on my fake "it's all good" face and go to my room.

For the next hour, my phone is surprisingly silent, and I'm glad. Not because I want to avoid anyone, I'm just not in the mood to hang out and pretend to be happy. It also gives me a chance to get some homework finished and out of the way.

But my small bit of silence is broken by a ringtone. It's not my phone, it's my mom's. I know whose special ringer that is too. I can't believe she talks to him. I throw down my pencil and head over to my door. I open in a small crack and listen in.

"No. He's not ready," My mom says. "I'm happy for you.

He doesn't know about it, though."

That gets me bolting from my room. "I don't know about what?"

My mom startles. "Jesus. Austin. How long have you been there?" The phone is still against her ear. I can hear mutters coming out of it, but I can't make out the words. "What is it?"

She frowns. "You want to talk to him?"

"No. You tell me. I don't want anything to do with him. As far as I'm concerned, he's dead to me."

My mom's eyes water. "Austin. I raised you better than that. Don't say things like that."

"I love you, Mom. But that one can kiss my ass."

"He's getting remarried."

That knocks the wind out of me. "What?"

Chapter Thirty

Adaline

I smack the vending machine with my palm. "Oh my God, just fork over my Kit-Kat bar, you murderous, dream-crushing hunk of metal!" I slap the glass again. My Kit-Kat remains wedged in place, and the machine ate my last dollar.

"Why is this happening today of all days?" I whine to no one in particular. I'm currently having my female moment in life, and chocolate makes it better. Of course, that chocolate would be better in my hand and entering my mouth instead of taunting me behind glass.

"Hey, Ads. What are you doing?" Austin asks.

Great. My crappy morning is about to get a whole lot worse. Ugh. I should have stayed home. Cramps are a valid excuse.

"Go away. I'm not in the mood."

"Emmm. Can't. Sorry. You look like you're in trouble. I want to offer my services," he says, flashing me his dazzling smile.

I want to be annoyed. I sigh. "My candy bar got stuck."

Austin laces his fingers together and extends out his arms, creating a sickening cracking noise. "I got this." He tilts the machine toward him then slams it back. Three items come loose and hit the bottom trap.

None of them are my candy bar, though. "Nice try. My candy is still in there clinging to the jaws of life."

"Hey, don't give up on my hero status just yet. I still got this." He pulls out a few dollars and inserts them into the feeder.

"Austin, stop. Don't you need that?"

He glares at me. "What? No." He presses the numbers and suddenly two Kit-Kats release. He bends down and digs out all the treasures then hands over both bars to me. "You're welcome."

Austin starts to walk away.

"Hey! I need to pay you back," I say instead of the thing I should say, which is "Thank you."

He laughs. "I don't need your cash." He continues to walk backward away from me. "Besides, consider it an early birthday gift. See you in history."

I'm about to tell him thank you, but he turns around and takes off. How is it possible that his simple gesture makes me feel like a total ass?

After school, I spot Austin making his way through the parking lot with a flock of girls trailing not far behind. I keep spying on him until I hear, "Addy, what are you doing?" Layla asks.

I turn my attention to Juliet's sister and fidget. "N-nothing."

"Reeeallly?"

I say nothing. She can't catch me in a total lie if I don't say anything. I feel a burn spread across my cheeks, though. Damn blushing.

"So, I didn't catch you zoning out in the parking lot?"

"Kind of."

She gives me a look that says she knows I'm full of it. "Anywho. Are you catching the bus, or would you like a lift?"

"Uh." I would like a ride, but Layla is possibly the worst driver on the planet. That's saying something because my mom is possibly a high contender on this list. Making it a reason I'm glad when my mom forgets to pick me up, and I dread asking her to.

"Tyler's driving," she says as if reading my thoughts.

Tyler seems like a safe driver, but I don't want to be stuck as the third wheel again. "I um … "

"Ads, get in," Austin says as he swings open the passenger door.

"Have a ride," I finish. Layla smiles.

"Nice. Have fun," she says.

I slide into Austin's car and shut the door. He slowly pulls out of the parking lot as I get my seatbelt fastened into place. "Thanks for the candy bar and, um, the ride home. You don't have to keep doing that."

"Right. Well, get used to it."

What's that supposed to mean? I'm a little offended now,

and I'm not sure why. Possibly how he said that. Possibly the words in general. I am so sick of him looking at me like I'm some kind of spoiled brat.

"We should talk about the project," I say.

Austin remains silent.

"I was thinking we could pick up the donations. I mean, unless you have to be somewhere."

We roll up to a stoplight, and he says, "Actually I do. I can't help anymore until Sunday."

"Wh-what? When were you going to tell me this? Austin, we've got nothing started. Just an idea, and that's not enough."

He turns a glare at me. "Adaline, you know sometimes people have more important shit going on than their freaking school work! I get you need this. I do, too, but I need to work a hell of a lot more than dealing with your stupid timelines and schedules!"

"You know what? I can walk from here. Thanks." I start to pull open the door.

"Shut the damn door, now!"

"Go to hell!" I hop out of his rust bucket and begin walking. Austin can't move forward unless he plans on breaking the law. I don't know what possessed me to hop out like I did. I hate walking. On top of that, these shoes are not very comfortable. Like at all. It's probably a good eight miles to my house too. Again, not the most brilliant idea on my part.

I'm not very far when a revved-up engine rolls up next to me. The window is down, and he shouts, "Stop being ridiculous! You're going to make me late."

I ignore him and keep walking. I realize I'm acting like

a total brat. I'm mad at him, though. He called my schedule stupid. He called my timelines stupid. He's the one who made me leader. I didn't want any of this. I knew one way or another I would be forced to work on this whole thing by myself. I thought for once maybe I was wrong, but nope, he proved me right. Asshole!

I get that he needs to work. He doesn't seem to understand that it's not just about the grade on this project that matters. It's the fact my mom is riding my case about everything. She thinks I'm falling behind, and this right here is making her case for her.

"You know what? I don't have time for this. If you want to act like this, fine."

I make the mistake of looking over at him. He pulls over and calls someone. "What are you doing? You can leave."

"Why? So I look like a total asshole? No! Hey … Can you swing by Sycamore Street?" he says.

"Who are you talking to?"

"Your ride. They'll be here in two minutes," he answers as he lowers his phone. "I'll wait until they get here."

I fold my arms. "Who was it?"

"Tyler."

I glare at him. "I don't need you to babysit me."

"Don't tick me off further, Adaline. I'm really not in the mood."

I should scream at him. Kick his tires. Something. I won't. His car would probably fall apart, and that would be all my fault. That's the last thing I need on my hands.

Tyler pulls up before I do something I severely regret. Layla looks at me from the passenger seat and says, "Ready?"

"Yes," I say and get into the back.

Tyler glances at me and then faces the road. "I've never seen Austin so wound up in all my life, Addy," he says following with a deep laugh.

"I didn't do anything." It's a total lie. I know I started the argument by yelling. He is at fault too. Maybe not as much, but again, I'm not going to admit that aloud.

Tyler takes me to my house. As soon as he pulls us into my driveway, I swing my door open and say, "Thanks."

"Hey, Addy. It's not my business or anything, but Austin is my boy. He cares for ya. Be a little easier on him," Tyler says.

I snort. "Tell your boy thanks for leaving me high and dry on this project. It's bad enough *her* best friend can't even bother showing up for anything. Then I got two ghosters, and now Austin is going to be MIA until Sunday. It's a real kick to my face."

Layla and Tyler exchange looks. I hop out and shut the door. I'm done. Everyone can stop thinking I'm the harsh one here. They want to flake off on this, fine by me; I'll do it all and make it look like they all helped. If those jokers think they're going to taint my grade, they seriously underestimated me.

Chapter Thirty-One

Austin

After work, I'm dog tired. I think about calling Adaline, though, and apologizing. At the same moment, I don't. She attacked me because I was honest. On top of that, there is the whole Greg thing. I'm not sure if they're together or not. I mean, she went to Tyler's party with him. He's always at her freaking lunch table.

Screw it. I need to know. I text her.

```
Me: U up?
```

It's only 9:00, but you never know. She might already be in bed.

```
Ads: Yeah.
Me: We need to talk.
Ads: No.
Me: Yes.
```

```
Ads: No, we do not!
Me: Yep we do.
```

I call her because I can see this is going to be difficult.

"What do you want?" she snaps off into the phone.

"Well, snippy, I want to know what time you want to start on Sunday? I can do double the work."

"I don't want your help. I ... " There is a loud screeching sound as if someone was peeling tires happening outside my house. "What was that?" she asks.

I laugh it off. "The TV. What did you think it was?"

"It sounded like someone is drag racing."

I laugh some more. "Yeah, who's gonna drag race? Mrs. Cumberman. She's 90 and has a cane. Although come to think about it, she does have that glint in her eyes that she secretly does donuts in the Swifty parking lot."

Adaline is giggling now. "Shut up! No, she doesn't. She's a sweet woman, Austin. Does she still have that pet raccoon?"

"Trouble? Nah he died."

"Aww." She pauses for a second then sighs, "Gosh, you're good. Distracting me from the fact I am upset with you, well, back to our conversation before you brought up Mrs. Cumberman. I don't need your help on the project."

I peek out the blinds in my room then snap them shut. I walk over to my bed and lay back against the sheets. "Ads, knock it off. You know you need all of us."

"Considering no one shows up, no I don't."

"None of them showed again?" I ask.

"No. I don't care. I've got this covered. Don't worry, everyone will get a good grade. I just realized I can't depend on you jerks in order to get a good grade."

"All right. Whatever." I hang up before I say something completely offensive.

The next few days all I do is school, work, homework, and sleep. I don't really talk much with my friends aside from the same typical lunch BS. Today is different. Tyler says, "You all right, man?"

"Fine. Why?"

"You haven't given a certain someone a ride home from school."

I shrug. "So? I'm not a taxi."

Tyler laughs. "Yeah. I know that. I could have sworn from my party that you were into her."

I glance away from my lunch and up at Tyler. "Why?"

"You really want to play this game?"

"Yeah."

"S'up?" Jared says as he drops into a chair next to Tyler. Juliet is beside him. What the heck is she doing over here?

Did I sit at the wrong table today? I look around the commons. Nope. I'm at the right table. "What's this?" I ask motioning to Juliet and Jared.

Jared raises a brow like "duh dude; it's my girlfriend. What's wrong with you today?" "She's allowed to sit with us."

"Never mind." I want to yell "no, she isn't." This is my table without the whole relationship crap clouding it. They've officially ruined lunch.

I shove everything in my bag and head into the library.

I've only been in here a few times, and all of those times were to find Adaline. When did I resort to eating my lunch in the library of all places? I walk over to a table in the back and slump down. I eat the rest of my things in peace and catch up on homework, that way I don't have as much after work.

As I'm working through my calculus, a strong scent of apples creeps up on me. I turn from my homework, and I see Adaline standing there. Arms folded and scowling, her glare rests on mine. "That's my table."

"I'm not doing this with you. Just sit over there." I point to the table across from mine.

She pouts. "It wobbles."

I sigh. "Fine. You win." I grab my things and move to the wobbly table. She stares at me. "What?"

"Why are you here of all places?" she asks.

I shrug. "I don't know."

"Do you really think my schedules are stupid?" she finally asks.

I look up at the ceiling. There are weird stains and patterns. Some look like someone took coffee and poured it all over.

Adaline is waiting for my response. Problem is, I don't know what to say. I have to remember that she's happy with Greg. I have to remember that she's mad at me for a lot of things.

I finally look over at her. "I don't think anything you do is stupid, Ads. I get this grade means a lot to you. But work means a lot to me. I need you to understand I'm not bailing on you. I just can't be there to help until Sunday. If we could figure out how we can put all this together using that one day that would be amazing."

"No one is showing up, though. What makes Sunday any different from all the other days? You ditched me last Sunday."

"Yeah. I know. But I got materials. So it's not like I totally wasn't working on the project."

She rolls her eyes. "Right. Whatever. You know most of the groups are almost finished. Juliet and Jared have hardly any time to spare with practice and whatever, and do you know their project is almost finished. Tyler and Layla, same thing. You know the only thing we have done is a barely thought out plan."

I want to argue with her, but she's right. Most of my friends are near complete on their projects, and shit, our group hasn't started anything.

"All right, Ads, what do you need me to do?"

Adaline opens her mouth then snaps it shut with a deep scowl. I'm about to ask what the heck is up with her face, but a soft voice says, "Hey, Austin. Mind if I share this table with you?" Before I can even answer the freshman from the party, Adaline slaps all her things together and leaves. I swear I can't win.

Chapter Thirty-Two

Adaline

I've been home for nearly an hour, and all I think about is school. Austin's pleading face. Ugh! I slam the meat mallet against the already flattened chicken breast. My mom grabs the mallet from me and smiles. "It's not always good to take your bad days out on your dinner. It won't be as tender and delicious."

I sigh. She's got a point. Dry chicken sucks. Still, using the mallet as a metaphorical device on an imaginary image of Austin's face makes me feel better. I shouldn't even care that he is so up and down and, well, all over the place. He frustrates me to no end. He seriously thinks we'll get a lot done in one day? He's dreaming! Then the brunette from the party has to come strolling into the library. She's tall, gorgeous, and dresses like all the girls he's ever dated before. So of course, I wouldn't stick around to hear him agree to share a table with her. I tried a new look following winter break after visiting my relatives and taking some pointers from my cousin, Sophie. I was uncomfortable in dresses, low cut shirts, and Uggs. All the effort didn't land me the guy I wanted anyway. Therefore I went back to my comf-zone of jeans and t-shirts.

"I think we're good here. Why don't you go see what your father is up to?" my mom says.

My dad usually hangs out in his study, reading books. He catches my eyes when I approach. "Whatcha reading?"

"It's about a man stuck in a different time period and trying to find his way back. It's interesting." He sticks a bookmark in the thick novel and sets it aside. "Why the frown?"

"I'm not ... I don't know. I feel so behind on this one thing, and I don't think I am going to catch up."

"Sit down. Tell me what it is, and maybe we can come up with a solution to help your time management skills."

This is why I love my dad, but I also didn't want to come in here. See, this nerdy time-tables scheduling I get from him. Call it an OCD-like trait if you will. However, it's not a favorite trait of others, more like an annoyance. "I got it mapped out. I um ... just have to stick to it."

I will never tell him how I'm in a group project, and my team has disappeared on me. I will never tell him that my grade is relying on them. He would totally flip and get my mom involved, and I've had enough of her butting into my life as it is. The last thing I want is her coming to my school and raising all kinds of drama.

"If you're sure, okay."

I plaster on a fake smile and nod. That's what good daughters do. They always look happy and bright even if their entire world around them is falling apart. The anxiety of losing my place in the advanced program as well as disappointing them is eating away at me bit by bit, and there is nothing I can do about it.

"I'm going to go help Mom set the table," I say.

My dad picks up his book again and says, "Sounds good."

As I am leaving his study, my phone rings. I stare at the caller ID.

"Hey Juls, what's up?"

"I've never had to ask you this before, so please don't get mad. Are you coming to the party I have set up for you on Saturday? I mean, it is one of the best friend's jobs, you know. To throw an epic birthday party for her bestie. If you aren't down with video games and chilling, though, I can totally do something else."

I head up to my room instead of in the dining area where I told my father I would be. I sigh into the receiver. "Can it just be us? Like, I know you are dating Jared. And I know you might want to hang out with your sister, too, but I don't want to have a party with all of them. In fact, I don't want a party at all." This is the thing about being super stressed out about everything around me. I tend to say things I don't mean. In truth, I like hanging out with people and having a good time. I'm just usually with people I want to hang out with. For example, Juliet and Chase. Now that Chase no longer wants to be my friend, it's rather depressing to just chill with Juliet. Especially since she'll more than likely bring up dating Jared and how awesome it is.

Call me selfish or even cowardly, but I do not want to have my celebrated day if her new love will overshadow me. Maybe I should try to get a boyfriend. Not Greg. But someone.

"Okay," Juliet says. "Are you still up for bowling then later in the evening?"

"On Saturday? I guess." I walk over to my desk and check out my reflection in my mini mirror. Gosh, I look like crap. Baggy eyes. *Is that a zit on my forehead?*

"It'll be fun. I promise. Girls versus boys."

A loud voice overtakes Juliet's, "That's right, girls rock! Wahooo!!!" I pull the phone back to give my ears a rest for a second.

I place it back and cringe. "Wait, is Rachel coming?"

Juliet laughs. "Uh. No. She has some crap to do, thank goodness."

"Well, who's all going again?"

"Jared, Tyler, Layla, Me duh, and Au … in."

"Who?"

She shouts, "What was that? Oh, okay. Hey, dinner is ready. Gotta go."

"Wait, what?"

The line is silent. I stare at the screen and scowl. Really? She thinks I'm stupid. She knows darn well I know she cooks all the meals in that house. If it's their mom, well it's not exactly edible. No, offense to Angela Valentine, but the first time I had a sleepover at Juliet's house after their dad died, I thought Ms. Valentine was trying to kill me. I asked Juliet later, "What was that we were supposed to be eating?" I remember she shrugged and told me she thought it was beef, but at this point, she wasn't sure.

Shortly after this Juliet started cooking most of the meals.

Occasionally there were pizza nights, but mostly her in the kitchen. So unless they ordered pizza, she's full of crap, and I can't believe she would do this to me.

I set my phone on my charger and hurry downstairs. It's not like anyone else will be calling me. I make my way into the dining room and start setting up the table. My mom comes into the room and says, "I think we should visit Paris again for spring break."

Chapter Thirty-Three

Austin

"I need the car in the morning. You're just going to have to take a bus," my mom says.

She could not have sprung worse news on me. I'm trying to keep up my status of not living on the shitball side of town. I had to divert Jared from dropping off my stack of video games he had in his room. I told him I'd come by later and get them.

Now this. I can't avoid this. I could lie about my wheels and say my last car got into an accident, and the car I have now was cheap enough to buy with the insurance claim money. I could easily lie about not being home so people didn't randomly drop by my old house expecting me. But this? This I can't lie about. I can't sit in front of my old house waiting for a ride. My mom is going in for an early shift at the diner which means she has to clock in at four in the morning. No offense to anyone who gets up at that time, but I sure as heck am not. I'm sleeping to my usual wake-up time, six.

I chew on my lower lip trying to think of how the hell I might pull this off. My mind is blank on ideas. I don't want to tell my mom the buses here don't run to the north side. The north side buses have their own schedule, and I would need to walk almost thirteen blocks to catch the one bus that goes to my school.

I simply agree and go directly into my room with a deep ache in my stomach. I never ever wanted my friends to know about this, but shit, it's time to face the music. Pulling out my cell from my back pocket, I call Jared. He's the only person I trust with this news. I know he won't say anything or make jokes about it. Tyler, on the other hand, has helped me out in a jam but might slip up to Layla about why they might be late or something.

Jared answers after two rings. Panting. "S'up?"

"Er … Did I interrupt something?"

"Nah. Juliet and I were running laps at the track. Don't tell her I said this, but she's kicking my ass."

I snort laugh. "Really? Is it worse than when coach makes us do that one training exercise challenge with the cross country team every year?"

"It's close. Real close. So what's up? I thought you were at work or something?"

I lean back against my bed. "Nope. Just got off early. My boss had to leave for some important meeting out of town. Closed up shop early, but tomorrow I'll be right back at it."

"Oh, cool. Want me to swing by then and drop those games off?"

I sigh. "About that. Look, I uh … I don't live there anymore."

"Um okay, since when?"

"Since about a few weeks ago."

He mutters something then says to me, "Really? And you didn't tell me until now, why?"

I squeeze my eyes shut. "Because it's embarrassing. Like straight bad."

"Like how bad? You live in the ghetto or something?"

I remain silent and he says, "Shit. For real?"

"Yeah, man. Look, I don't want any judgment. I'll explain most of this later. I need a favor, though, aside from you not telling a soul about this."

"Name it, man."

"I need a ride tomorrow and probably like every day for this week."

Jared doesn't even hesitate. "Done. Text me the address. I'll see you in the morning. But Austin, you're going to have to run with me. And you need to tell Tyler. Not now, but eventually. We're like brothers for life."

"I know. It's just embarrassing."

"I get it. Not exactly, but I can picture it. We have each other's backs, though. Don't worry, I won't say a word. That's on you."

Relief washes over me. "Thanks, man." We hang up, and I text him my dirty secret.

He doesn't send back laughing emojis or anything. He just says okay.

"Wow. This is … wow," Jared says the next morning outside my house.

"A shit hole. I know."

"You didn't wreck your car, did you?"

I slide into his truck and shake my head. "Nope. Had to sell it to help pay some bills."

"Damn, dude. I had no idea it was like this." We pull away from the street and make a turn at the first stop sign.

Of course, he didn't know how bad things were. I didn't want anyone to know. I wanted to keep this from everyone because why should they care about what is happening to me? They've got their own shit to worry about. Jared's got his dad always riding his case about something or other. That seems normal, though. I mean, his dad is the athletic director as well as the football coach of our school. Tyler's parents, well, those two are crazy.

"So, is this why you've been ditching Adaline?"

What? She told him this? I'm going to lay into her at school. All this pressure from both sides. She needs to get it through her thick skull I can only do so much. "I didn't. I told her I could only help on Sundays. You would think I have stabbed her or something the way she got ticked off at me. I get she has all these crazy timelines and shit, but she needs to understand not everyone works this way."

Jared snorts as he drives over a set of railroad tracks. "What about the others? My group is almost done with our project."

I almost want to say, "Good for him. What's he want? A freaking cookie?" But I can't. Because he's helping me out, and he's not saying this to rub it in my face. He's telling me this because clearly my group sucks, and there needs to be someone taking charge. Making sure everyone is helping Adaline if I can't be there. Group effort.

"I am going to have a chat with everyone today."

"Good. Juliet is looking to maim you. She thinks you are purposely screwing Addy over."

I shrug. "I'm not. I can't tell Adaline what happen to me. I didn't even want to tell you."

"I get it. But you gotta get the others to help or something."

I nod. "I'll work on it. We really did get stuck with the shit end of the group, though."

Jared agrees. The remainder of the car ride to school we listen to tunes on the radio.

When we pull into the school, Juliet marches over to Jared's truck and points at me, "I'm mad at you, Austin."

"I heard," I say. "I'll fix it."

She smiles. "You better."

Jared walks her into the school, and I wait a few minutes before I enter. I need to make a plan, one that can fix this project and possibly make things right with Adaline.

Chapter Thirty-Four

Adaline

"You told me you would go," Juliet complains before she takes a huge bite of her sandwich.

"I can't go out because I got stuck working with absolute, self-absorbed idiots."

"Didn't you talk to Austin?" she asks. The question causes me to sputter my drink.

I cough a few times trying to clear my throat. "Why?"

She shrugs. I cannot believe she ratted me out to Jared who probably gave Austin some crappy pep-talk or whatever. She's supposed to be my friend. She's supposed to keep what I complain about to herself and not tell her darn boyfriend about it.

"You're mad at me aren't you?" she asks.

I almost want to ask her what on earth gave her that impression. Instead of giving her a piece of my mind I say, "I have it handled. I don't need Austin or anyone for that matter."

"What are you talking about?" Juliet asks.

"It's exactly as I said. They never stick to the plans set forth, so I don't need them."

Her expression turns worrisome. "You can't do that project by yourself and slap their names on it, Addy. You have to have physical proof they were helping you." She snorts. "I mean, what are you going to do? Videotape and clip them into your video report?"

I say nothing. That's exactly what I plan on doing.

She latches on to my arm and shakes her head. "Oh, my God, Adaline! That's cheating. You would never ever cheat on anything in your entire life. Please tell me that's not what you plan on doing."

I refuse to answer her because along with never being a cheater, I don't make it a habit of lying to my friends. Instead, I get up from the lunch table and go straight to my next class.

I intended on waiting out in the hall on the dirty floor. The art room is open, so I step in. "Mrs. Clegge?"

The tall blond woman in her early thirties steps out of the kiln and says, "Adaline, shouldn't you be at lunch?" She shuts the door and presses some buttons on the wall.

I nod. "Yeah. I needed to catch up on the last assignment you gave us."

She turns and smiles, showing off her crooked teeth with a small bit of lipstick staining them. "All right then. Please go to your seat. I need to run up to the office for a few items. Do not touch anything, especially that door." She points to the kiln.

I pull out my things from my bag. I open my book and flip through the sketches. Most of them happen to be of Austin or some form of him. Images of him seem to cloud my mind. It's not like he ever actually sat in front of me and let me sketch him. I should rip all of these out and burn them.

I go to the page I was working on. It's not of Austin, thank goodness. The assignment Mrs. Clegge gave us was to draw a detailed scenic landscape. We needed to have the following items in our sketch: trees, houses, livestock, and a body of water of some sort. I decided to draw a field with trees edging both sides of the paper. A few houses in the distance, along with horses, and a stream. I'm just fleshing out the details and making everything stronger.

My drawing has my full attention, so I don't notice a shadow casting over my shoulder until I turn and startle. "Good lord! Greg, what is the matter with you? Warn a girl; don't just stare down at her."

"Sorry. I noticed you were in a zone, and I didn't want to bother you. I needed to talk to you, though."

I kick out a chair across from me and say, "Sit."

He walks around the table and takes the seat, which kind of surprises me because I thought for sure he would try for the seat next to me. I mean, he is always doing that sort of thing. He plops down and sighs.

I wait for him to start, but he's just staring at me. "Um, you wanted something?"

"I did. This Saturday for your party … I was wondering if we could maybe go as a couple?" Greg asks.

The tip of my pencil snaps, leaving a dark spot on my tree which I won't get out gracefully with a simple touch of the eraser. This is exactly what I did not want happening. This right here. Greg pulling a total one-eighty on me and flipping this into a Chase situation.

I need to quit stalling and give him an answer. My pause is drawing out longer than necessary. "I uh … I uh … "

As if by magic, Mrs. Clegge returns. I want to haul out of my seat, run to her, and throw my arms around her for saving me from embarrassment. I won't because that would be weird. I also won't because I'll probably get detention. Mrs. Clegge has a space policy, breaking it means she slaps you with detention. Frankie Holten, a girl in my grade, made the mistake of giving Mrs. Clegge a hug when she said she was entering her art in a young artist competition in town. Mrs. Clegge let her work still enter, but the girl had three days' detention.

"Excuse me, are you supposed to be somewhere right now, young man? Adaline, I didn't think I needed to stress about rule ten in my classroom, but no visitors. Leave them outside the door."

I wince because if I get a detention over this, I'm going to kill Greg.

"Oh, I'm sorry, Mrs. Clegge. I didn't realize you had those kinds of rules. It's still lunchtime, so I didn't think it mattered," Greg says.

I squeeze my eyes shut. *Go away. Just stop talking and leave.* He carries on, "Would it be okay if I took her out in the hallway and spoke with her?"

"Greg," I say with a glare directed at him. "We can talk later, like after school. Okay?" What I really mean: he'll call, and I'll ignore it because there is no way I'm doing this again. No way!

"Young man?" Mrs. Clegge says as she points to the door. "You must leave my classroom at once."

"Got it!" He snaps. He stomps out of the room, and I sigh with relief.

Mrs. Clegge looks at me, mouth in a grim line. "I like you, Adaline, so I'm going to give you a warning. But next time I will have you stay after school and help me clean all the pottery wheels as well as the floors."

Ugh. "I'm sorry, Mrs. Clegge, it really won't happen again."

"See that it doesn't." She walks over to her desk and sits. There is a row of projects lined up on the long table next to her desk. She picks up a vase, sneers, and places it back. Then she marks something in her grade book and moves on to the next piece. I watch her do this two more times before I return to my sketch in front of me.

The dark pencil mark I'll work on correcting later, much like my life.

Chapter Thirty-Five

Austin

"Did you talk to her yet?" Jared asks as I get into his truck.

"No. There was no time. I was going to during history, but Mrs. Dinger decided today would be a test day. At lunch, she vanished. So, no."

He shakes his head and starts his truck. The engine roars to life. "Can you drop me off at Harvey's shop?"

"You work there?"

I nod.

"You know that's Juliet's uncle? He's nice, but he's also scary as shit. I was over at Juliet's house, and she was making cookies. Anyway, he stopped over for something, saw me, and started telling me stories about how he had to kill a man before. If I ever hurt Juliet, no one would be able to find me."

I don't know why, but I laugh. Hard, deep in the belly laugh. "He said that?"

Jared turns us down a street and growls, "It's not funny.

I'm dead serious. He scared the crap out of me. Juliet keeps telling me he was messing with me, but you didn't see the look on his face."

"Right. Well, I'm not worried about him hurting me. I'm not dating any of his relatives." I pick through my bag and pull out my work clothes. "Thanks again for this. I get paid Friday, so I'll spot you some gas money."

"Dude, don't. It's fine," he says.

"Yeah, I'm still giving it to you. I don't want charity."

Jared parks his truck at Harvey's and scowls at me. "This isn't charity. This is what friends do. You'd know that if you just told me or even Tyler before now what the hell was going on."

I whip the seatbelt off and snap. "Really? Because you and Tyler would totally understand. Newsflash, you two both don't have to work. Shit, Tyler probably won't ever have a job because he's freaking loaded and a trust fund kid. Your dad would break every bone in your body before he'd let you work because he's looking for you to go off to the NFL." I shake my head. "But me, I probably won't even be able to go to a big ten school. Not without a scholarship and some way to support my mom on top of that. There's no way. So I'm sorry for not letting you and everyone else into my mess."

"That's your whole problem, Austin. If you would have told me sooner, my dad could have found a way to help you and your mom. I don't know what, but I know he did it before with Stevenson. He's over at OSU now."

I roll my eyes. "Whatever man, thanks for the lift." I get out before I say something I'll regret later. Jared's cool. So is Tyler, but I don't need to be looked at like a charity. I'm going to earn enough working on these damn cars that I can move us to a decent house. Or at least have some put aside to move my mom and me into a decent apartment somewhere.

I walk into the shop and head to the restroom to change. Once I'm out, Harvey spots me and gives me a nod. "Was that my niece's boyfriend?"

"Yep. Heard you scared the crap out of him," I say with a chuckle.

He laughs too. "I was giving him my pep talk. I don't want anyone thinking they can crush my girls' hearts and not answer for them."

I'd hate to see what he did to Mark then or even Adam.

"I got a car for you. You ready?" Harvey asks.

I nod, and he walks me into the pit. "See that on lift four?" he asks.

It's a 1969 Camaro. Cherry with chrome handles. It's freaking gorgeous. "I do."

"You'll be working on her today." He hands me a list of things it is to have done to it: regular maintenance from the oil change to tires rotated. I'm also supposed to look at all the fluids and top them off.

The inner car geek in me gets excited, and I practically hop over to the spot. As I'm getting ready to slide under the classic beauty, my phone buzzes in my pocket. Harvey has a strict no calls in the pit policy, so I hit ignore without even looking who's trying to get ahold of me. My phone goes off two more times, and this time I glance at the caller ID. Adaline.

I don't have time for this. I need to talk to her, wanted to all day, but she can wait.

It's around nine when I ring Adaline back.

She deeply yawns into the phone and says, "Hello."

"What did you need, sunshine?"

"Ugh. Listen, I figured out how to make everyone happy. I'll just do everything and paste you all into the video."

I slap my door to my bedroom shut. "No! Ads what is the big deal? Why can't you wait until Sunday? I told you I can be there to help on Sunday."

"Take it or leave it. I've got plans, and I won't spend spring break doing this project. In fact, I won't spend another moment waiting on you jerks to show up. I've got most of it put together anyway."

She did what? I'm so mad. Not really at her, but the others for putting her in this position. I'm also mad at myself. I can't fix a darn thing, though.

"I'm really tired, so I'm going to hang up now," she says.

"Please don't."

"Austin … " She whispers my name as if it was glass cutting her.

I lay against my mattress. "Ads, I have a few hours on Saturday. Can I stop by?"

"It's my birthday."

That she says this like I have no clue it's her birthday, kills me. Of course, it's her birthday. I know because it's a few days after mine. "Yeah. I know."

"Well, I will probably be out with Greg."

"Greg?" What the hell! She's going to be out with him? I didn't even give her a time. I don't know if she's trying to make me jealous or if she is blowing me off. Either way, I'm super pissed.

"Yes, Greg. Why does it matter?" her voice sounds sharp like she's no longer exhausted.

I grip my phone tighter. "I think you're full of shit!"

"I am not!"

"The hell you aren't. I didn't even give you a time. Whatever. Have fun with Greg!" I turn my phone off and place it on the charger. I press my head against my pillows and growl, "Freaking Greg!"

Chapter Thirty-Six

Adaline

I didn't want to tell Austin I was hanging out with Greg. I just didn't want him coming over here. Not on my birthday. Not when I'm trying everything in the world to forget him. It's impossibly hard, too, because all I do is think about him.

When Greg asked me to go to the bowling event like we were on a date, my first thought was, *Why can't Austin be asking me this? Not Greg.* That right there is a huge problem. Clearly, Austin doesn't care about me that way because all he seems to do is ditch me. Really, what else am I supposed to expect? He did it to me before, has done it several times. As soon as I feel us getting close, he pumps the brakes.

I just hope he hasn't asked Greg if we're dating or anything. That will be humiliating if I have to explain to Greg how I'm not interested in him in that way, on top of possibly seeing Austin gloating because he was right about something. I would rather have someone sell off all my organs than have that happen.

As I step into school the following day, the cool air conditioning bathes my face, and goosebumps spread over my body. Chase storms up to me, grabs my hand, and pulls me into the library before I can even register what's going on. "Chase, what the heck?"

"Shhh! I talk. You listen." He takes us to a table and points to a chair. "Sit."

"I will not. You have no right to just drag me wherever you want."

He frowns. "I know. This is important. Like you need to know this now."

I roll my eyes and take a seat. It's the least I can do after the ordeal I probably put him through. "Thank you." He takes the seat next to me and says, "You need to stop hanging out with Greg as soon as possible."

"Really, why?"

"Adaline!" He snaps. Someone shushes him, and he growls, "Oh, you shush! The bell hasn't even rung yet." He turns back to me. "He thinks he has a shot to get in your pants. In fact, he told practically the whole locker room this during lifting. Austin came in late, so he missed it, but I know for a fact, Adaline, he would have put Greg in a locker if he caught wind of it. I'm warning you now, stay away from that guy."

I scowl at Chase. "Seriously Chase? Not only are you a world class asshole right now for even telling me this in the library, but you could have called me about this last night. And the fact you mention that if Austin would have heard anything makes me want to punch you. I don't want Austin defending me. In fact, I want nothing more than to forget the guy. So if Greg thinks he can get in my pants, then okay."

"What?" Chase's eyes widen. He looks as if I slapped him.

I stand up. "Thanks. Really. Thanks for the warning and all, but if you truly cared, you would have told me this as soon as you heard it, not a day later." I stomp out of the library in a foul mood.

I find Greg waiting by my locker. I don't even give him the time of day. "The answer is no way in hell," I pop off before spinning my combo into my locker.

"What? Why?"

"Get moving, Greg, before you lose a finger or an eye; I haven't decided yet." I grab my books from my locker, ready to shut it.

Greg is sputtering beside me. "D-did … It was a joke. I wasn't being serious."

"Getting into my pants is a joke now? Oh, I'm sorry. Please tell me when I should stop laughing." I remain silent and glare at him.

"Okay," he raises his hands. "I'm sorry. I shouldn't have said anything. I just … I really like you, and I thought if people knew I was into you, well, you'd say yes. Because no one else would ask you out."

I slap my locker closed and storm past him. Of all the nerve. I mean, seriously. I should go back and smack him across his face.

As I'm working my way to my first-period class, I spot Austin. That freshman is walking with him. Instead of going to class as planned, I march right over to him and jab my finger into his chest. "If you aren't at my house Saturday morning, I'm going to make sure we all fail!"

"Whoa. Ads." He has that smirk, the one that makes my heart go crazy because my heart is stupid. It doesn't listen to my brain whatsoever. "Good morning to you too."

"Uh, I guess I'll talk to you later," the freshman says.

He doesn't look at her, though; his eyes are focused on mine. "Yeah, okay," he says. "So, sunshine, what's up with you poking me in the chest? Thought you were busy Saturday with Greg." The way he says his name, I sense a slight edge in his voice.

"I'm no longer talking to him. Not that that's any of your business."

"Hmm, well, color me curious. Why not?" he asks as he turns me around and loops his arm through mine.

"What are you doing?" I ask. Not that I really mind. Well, my brain does but my body doesn't.

He walks us down to his locker while he says, "We're walking. I can't have you running off now, can I?" He winks at me.

"My class is back that way," I nudge my head in the opposite direction.

"I know where your classes are. This is only going to take a second, and we can walk you to your class first."

"But you'll be late."

He shrugs. "Yeah, and it's not the end of the world if I am." He pops open his locker and grabs a few things. Puts them in his bag and shuts the door. He proceeds to walk us back to my class.

"So why aren't you talking to Greg?" he asks.

My cheeks burn. I don't know why I'm blushing. I'm not going to tell him the reason why. It's none of his business.

"Silence," he says. "Really?"

"I told you before, it's none of your business."

He sighs. "All right, it's none of my business." We turn a corner, and suddenly he swings me into a set of lockers. Just my back hits. He caresses my head with his hands, and then his lips press against mine.

When he pulls back, he says, "I need that. The next person you're going to date is me, Adaline. Not Greg, not some weirdo from band or whatever. It's going to be me."

I feel like my entire body turns to mush, and this is some twisted dream. But my back feels the cool metal against it. My fingers feel his slight stubble jawline. So this can't be a dream. Right?

He smiles and takes my hand then walks me the rest of the way to class. Everything from this moment on is such a daze. I barely hear the tardy bell ring or know how I even got to my seat. What's happening?

"Adaline?" Mrs. Larken calls.

"I'm here."

"We established that during attendance. Can you please answer the question?"

Question? What? Crap. See? This is what Austin does to me. This can not happen again. No more kissing that boy. He's turning me into a total mess.

Chapter Thirty-Seven

Austin

I'm on cloud nine. Hell, I could practically skip through the halls. I'm not, but I could.

I think my kiss stunned Adaline, though. She was walking into class like a zombie or a robot going through the motions but not really all there. I hope she's okay. I mean, I did have to leave and get to my own class, which is at the other end of the school, in less than a minute.

I barely made it before the bell rang. Mr. Walden tapped his watch and said, "Cutting it kind of close there, Austin, don't you think?"

"Yeah. Sorry." I'm really not. If being late meant kissing Adaline again, oh yeah, I would be late for every single class for the rest of this year and my senior year.

"Take a seat."

Trent hisses, "Hey man, sorry about your girl."

I slide into my seat near the back. "What are you talking about?"

"Frost. Heard she gave up her goods to Greg. Don't you have lifting the same time with him?"

I laugh. "He didn't get shit." If Greg or anyone tells another soul that, I'm going to kick their sorry ass.

He doesn't say another word, but the entire time I'm in class all I can think about is how Adaline changed her mind about hanging out with Greg. Did they really do something?

Tyler jabs me in my stomach. "Dude, what's up with you? Where are your catlike reflexes?"

I slap him upside his head as we make our way through the parking lot. "Where's yours?"

"Funny. Why do you have Jared giving you a ride? You know your house is on my way, not his."

Jared is not even outside yet. This is also the first time that Tyler has spotted me getting a ride from Jared. Shit. Before I can even say anything, Layla walks up to his Jeep. Tyler usually opens the door for her, but he is still standing there waiting for me to say something.

"Are we not leaving yet?" Layla asks.

"In a second, babe, I want to know why Austin here didn't even ask if I would pick him up. I thought we were bros."

I roll my eyes. "I thought you wanted the alone time with Layla, and I don't want to be a backseat man."

Tyler shrugs. "Fair enough. So what's up with you and Frost? I saw you pressing her against the lockers this morning. I was going to ask you about it in lunch, but you weren't even in there."

Yeah, I was up in the library. I was holding a small meeting without Adaline to get our group on board and helping. It was a waste. Rachel didn't bother showing. Zander was there one second, gone the next. Lucas well, hell, the dude fell asleep.

"Nothing is up with me and Frost," I say.

I hear a small gasp behind me, and then something smacks the back of my shoulder. I turn, and there is Adaline with wide eyes and Juliet holding a shoe in one hand with her arms folded. Jared, of course, is staring at me like I half lost my mind.

I take a step toward Adaline. "I didn't mean it like that, Ads."

She backs up. "Don't come near me, Austin."

"Adaline, seriously, we're not dating yet. That's what I meant."

My shoulder gets smacked again. I turn to Juliet. "Knock that shit off!"

"Absolutely not. You hurt my friend, and I get to hurt you. Simple as that. What are you looking at Jared for? He's not going to stop me," Juliet snaps.

"You know what? Forget it." I turn and start walking away from everyone. The school. Adaline. My friends. I don't give a shit. I'm sick of trying to explain things, and it comes out wrong. I'm just flat-out done.

Chapter Thirty-Eight

Adaline

A few days have passed since I overheard Austin basically say we weren't anything. I mean, I guess his earth-shattering kisses are an everyday occurrence and mean nothing. But they don't happen every day to me.

It's my birthday, and I plan on spending most of it in my bed. I should work on the project, but I've given up on it. At this point, I don't care if I am pulled from the advanced program. My mom will be upset with me, but so what? I don't care.

There is a knock on my door. "Adaline, are you up?" my mom says before the covers over my head are being ripped from me.

"Yes," I grumble.

"Well, happy birthday. You have spent most of the morning in bed. I wanted to take you out for a birthday lunch since I couldn't get time away to take you out yesterday."

I shuffle out of bed and make my way to my closet. "Is it

a nice place, or can I just wear whatever?" I ask.

"I was hoping a nice place, but it's your birthday. You choose."

Choices. Ugh. "I don't care."

"Please, I want this to be your decision. You never seem to decide things."

I drop down to the floor and start crying. "Oh, honey. What's wrong?" she asks as she drops beside me and hugs me.

"I don't want to choose a place to eat. I don't even want to choose a college. I'm scared I'll pick the wrong thing. I'm always picking the wrong things," I cry out.

"Oh, Addy. No. I'm sorry you feel so pressured. That wasn't my intention. I just always want what is best for you." She rubs my back, and as soothing as it is, her words are doing a better job. "I didn't want you to have a dream school in mind like Sophie did but just put it off until the last minute. Only to have your heart crushed because you were waitlisted or something. I wanted you to be able to have the best chances possible."

"What if I don't want to go?" I look over at her, tears blurring my vision. "What if I want to take a year and explore the world?"

"Is that what you want to do?"

I nod. "I just ... I wanna see things before I'm stuck behind books, lectures, and have to do a bunch of assignments."

She takes a deep breath. "Okay. So do you know what you want to eat?"

I laugh and wipe away stray tears. "Yeah. Chinese."

"All right. Go get ready, nice clothes, and I'll meet you downstairs.

Once she leaves, I enter my bathroom and take a shower. As I'm brushing my teeth, I hear a tapping followed by "Shit!" I step out of my bathroom wrapped in my towel, toothbrush still in my mouth, and look over at my balcony.

Austin is there with a wrapped box in hand.

I march right over to the door and open it. "Whaaa ooo wat?"

"Damn it! Why are you answering the door in a towel?" He guides me farther into my room and shuts the balcony door. He also draws the curtains as if someone could actually see into my window.

I walk into my bathroom, spit my toothpaste out, and then rinse. I can't believe I answered the door looking like a foaming rabid dog. I tighten the towel around me and enter my room again. He's sitting at my desk, gift in hand, spinning around in my chair.

"What are you doing here, Austin?"

He stops spinning and looks up at me then back at the floor. "I can't talk to you while you're naked, Ads. I can't. Go put clothes on."

"I'm not naked."

"Under that towel you're naked, are you not? One slip and I'll lose my mind. Please go put some clothes on."

The wicked part of me kicks in. "You mean like this," I tease pretending to unravel the towel. Austin shifts the chair away so fast it almost gives me whiplash.

He faces the desk and puts his head down. "I swear you are trying to push me."

"Maybe I am. Maybe you deserve it." I make my way to my closet and change. Not because he asked me to but because my mom is waiting downstairs, and I need him to leave.

I throw on a skirt and a white silk button down. I clear my throat and say, "I'm done."

He spins around and growls. "That's worse than the towel. Are you trying to kill me over here?"

I ignore him. "Whatever. What are you doing here? I told you not to."

He stands up and walks over to me. He drops the gift on the bed and says, "I know what you said. But when have I ever listened?"

"I can't do this. You can't come in here, say things like that, and then shrug it off like it's no big deal. Just go. And please use the front door next time." I leave him in my room. Probably not the best idea, but I needed to leave. I want him, but I can't do these games. Not anymore.

I grab my purse from the rack and meet my mom in the kitchen.

She looks over at me from the breakfast nook. "Ready?"

"Yep."

Chapter Thirty-Nine

Austin

I don't know if I'm flattered or pissed. I mean, she just left me in her room. I go over to her desk and grab a piece of paper from her drawer. Then I write a note to her. Once I'm finished I place it by the box and leave her room.

After I climb down the tree leading to her balcony, I get into my car and drive over to the shop. I'm glad my mom didn't need it today. Otherwise, my little trip to Adaline's house would never have happened.

I still can't believe she greeted me in nothing but a towel and a flipping toothbrush in her mouth. God, the ideas that flowed through my head were going to drive me nuts. I mean, everything about her drives me nuts, but that right there? That was blue balls' central territory.

Harvey was awesome enough to give me today off after I explained to him about our class project. So he agreed to let me work Monday through Friday and give me the next three Saturdays off. I didn't want that much time off, but hey, this project obviously isn't going to do itself.

I drive over to Rachel's house and ring the doorbell. Her father answers. "We don't want whatever you're selling."

"I'm here to see Rachel, sir."

He glares at me. "Rachel! You better not be dating this boy that's at the door!"

I should say I am dating her, and we're going to run away together, just to give this dude hives. I don't. I can't have Rachel overhearing this and something terrible happening. Like her take me seriously, or Adaline find out, and I never hear the end of it.

Rachel comes to the door, rubbing her eyes, hair all crazy. "What? Austin, dude … " she yawns. "What time is it?"

"It's freaking noon, Rach. Look, I need help. Go get dressed, and I'll get us coffee on the way."

She peers out the door and spots my car. "I'm driving. I'm not getting in that thing you call a car."

"Whatever."

I lock it, and she laughs. "No one is going to steal that thing."

She lets me inside and tells me to wait in the living room. I do, for a whole hour. Did she fall and hit her head? Hell if I know. Her father comes into the room and says, "Is she getting changed?"

I nod.

"How long have you been here?"

"An hour," I answer.

He snorts. "Yeah, you'll probably be here for another one. What are your intentions with my daughter if I may ask?"

I shrug. "I was just getting her to help on the school project we have."

He takes a seat near me and flips through different stations until he lands on the stock market. "School project, you say? Rachel hasn't mentioned any projects aside from decorating prom."

I refrain from rolling my eyes. Of course, she wouldn't. Rachel loves anything that puts the attention on her. Since this school project doesn't do that, she doesn't care about showing up.

He sighs. "I'm sorry for snapping earlier. She brought some riffraff home the other night covered in tattoos and piercings. She knows I can't have that going on with my campaign running. My competition would have a field day."

I shrug again. "It's no big deal. We're going to be doing some drilling and hammering, so I wasn't going to wear nice clothes for that."

"Nope. Don't need to ruin good clothes. So what is the project?"

"We're building a library nook in the park and calling it Bookworm Station."

He turns from the TV and smiles at me. "That's really interesting. Do you have all the materials for this?"

"Nope. We have to go pick up supplies. See if anyone wants to donate lumber and whatever."

He shakes his head. "No. If they don't donate, let me handle it. Just keep me informed on when it's done."

"Oh, okay." I don't think we're supposed to use our project as a campaign piece but whatever. He wants to supply the materials, that's good enough for me.

Rachel finally enters. "We're out. Be back later," she says.

"Use the card I gave you to get the supplies, Rachel," her dad says.

She rolls her eyes. "Yeah. Okay."

She pulls me from the seat and leads me to the garage. She walks over to her black Mustang and says, "Get in."

Rachel drives us all over town. Not one of them is the lumber store.

"We need to go to the lumber yard. Now."

"Fine. What has your boxers in a twist?"

I scowl. "I want to get this class shit done, so I can go back to other things."

She laughs. "Honestly, I don't know why you're so worried. Frosty Queen said she was doing it all the other day."

"Don't call her that. Ever. And she isn't doing shit. We're all doing this no matter what."

"What is with you lately?" She whips us around a bend so fast I almost lose my balance.

"Could you take it easy? Jesus, I don't want to die on the way there."

She slows down a tad. "There. You happy?"

"Very." I shake my head.

"You know, avoiding the question about Frost doesn't mean I forgot. You like her, huh? She's the reason you agreed to go with me to the dance, isn't she?"

I scrub a hand over my face. "Yeah. I'm sorry. I should have told you."

"Don't. I wanted to make someone jealous, too, but it backfired."

I laugh. "Who?"

She pulls us into Lumberjacks and says, "I'm not saying."

We walk into the store, and I say, "We're going to need a truck if we're getting the lumber today."

"Call Jared or Tyler. I'm sure one of them can help," Rachel says as she grabs a cart.

I can't call my friends. This needs to be all of us helping. I call Zander.

"Bro … it's not past three," he says.

"You got a truck or someone who will let us borrow a truck?"

"Where am I going?"

"Lumberjacks. Thirty minutes."

"Fine."

Maybe if I'm lucky, we can get this done today.

Chapter Forty

Adaline

After lunch, my mom drives us back to our house. I go up to my room hoping that Austin is no longer there.

He isn't. His gift is, along with a note. I set them aside because I can't look at this right now.

I change into some crap clothes and head into my garage where I have all the parts to make the book nooks. My dad helped me saw the pieces last night after dinner. All I need to do is put it together, stain it, and set it up in the park.

I'm interrupted by my best friend. "Happy Birthday!" she says in an excited, almost-like scream in her voice.

I turn from my wooden pieces and nod. "Hey."

She drops her gift and frowns. "Oh man, you're not even dressed. You didn't forget, did you? Whoa."

"As you can see, I'm sort of trying to get this done. My mom wants to take us to Paris on spring break. I'm pretty sure I won't be able to take this with me on the plane."

She raises a brow. "Seriously? No. You aren't doing this

by yourself. God, so help me, I can't believe I am saying this. I'll help you, but only because I totally love you as a friend, and it's your birthday. Give me three minutes. I'm going to change into some crap clothes from your stash."

"Bottom drawer in the closet has all my paint wear. Thanks a lot, Juls."

She leaves the garage, and I continue to nail the pieces. Juliet is taking forever. Heck, I might be finished by the time she returns. I hear a hard pounding on my garage door. I push the button. As the door is rising, I notice three sets of shoes.

Tyler walks in, looks around my little studio and says, "Happy birthday, Addy. I heard you needed these muscles."

"Uh, what are you doing here?" I ask. I look over at Layla, and she is just shaking her head.

She playfully slaps Tyler's arm and says, "Stop that. You're being goofy."

Jared steps into my studio and takes the hammer and nails from me. "We're told you need help. And since you need an extra set of hands, Juliet can film all of us helping from the forearms down."

Layla rolls her eyes. "In that whole roundabout way, we're here to help you cheat."

"Oh," I say and laugh. "You guys rock. Thanks."

"It was Juliet's idea, which is totally unlike my sister," Layla says with a smirk.

"I know. All these bad influences are finally rubbing off on the girl. Hey, that means you're next, buddy," Tyler jokes as he points to Jared.

Juliet walks into the garage in my paint bibs and shirt.

"Wow, you look amazing," Jared says.

If they start making out, I'm taking this wood and running.

Tyler bumps into my art easel, and my sketchbook falls off. He goes to pick it up, and I hurl toward him. I'm too late. He swoops it up and laughs, "Oh, wow. This is like a spitting image of Reed, isn't it?" He shows the room and my cheeks burn.

"Wow. Austin told us you were good, Addy, but damn," Jared says as he drops the hammer and nails on the table and grabs the sketchbook from Tyler. He goes through the pages.

"Thanks. Wait, Austin talked about my art?" I ask.

He nods. "Yeah. A few times."

I have no idea how I feel about that information. I mean, I like it, I also don't. I need to forget about Austin. These types of things are not helping. Next year we will be seniors and then off to God knows where. A relationship with a boy who is so hot and cold all the time is the last thing I need to add to my already full plate.

"Give us direction, Addy," Juliet says. "Let's get this built so we can go bowling."

Here goes nothing, I hope I can pull this off.

Chapter Forty-One

Austin

Rachel films us gathering the material. We swap her phone between all of us, and then I say, "Adaline is at the garage prepping the layouts while we get the materials."

I make a point to include Adaline in each bit. Zander and Lucas are barely any help, but we make sure to include them. After our trip to the hardware store, we head over to the park.

"What the hell is this?" Rachel asks as she points to a big book nook.

I look around the area and curse. Adaline must be behind this. Damn it!

I'm pissed. I dial her number, but it goes directly to voicemail.

"What the hell is this? I told you to wait. Call me," I snap off, then I end the call.

"I thought you told me she needed help!" Rachel yells. "This looks finished to me, and I just wasted a Saturday for what?"

"You didn't waste anything. We're going to change things up. We'll make it an entertainment center. Adaline is always complaining about how you can never show off your work in the city. Not without being called a vandal and whatever. So we're going to make it. Right here by the book nook," I say.

Hopefully, this will be my forgiveness gift to her too.

"Hey, are you coming out bowling tonight?" Jared asks.

"I wasn't planning on it," I say into my phone.

"You need to."

"Fine. What time?"

"Seven."

I agree and hang up the phone. I glance at the clock in the kitchen. It's 6:20 right now. I trudge my way to the bathroom and grab a quick shower. After I get dressed, I do the essentials: deodorant, spray, and put some product in my hair. I can't go out looking like a total bum even if I feel like one.

I go to grab the keys, but they aren't on the counter where I left them. "Mom?"

"Austin?"

"Do you have the keys?"

She nods. "Did you need them for something?"

"I got a thing," I say.

She places her hands on her hips. "A thing? Like what's that, a party?"

I have to be careful what I say here. If I say I'm going out bowling, she is going to assume I'm spending money we shouldn't. Instead, I say, "Just hanging with some friends."

"Can't I just drop you off? I need the car tonight."

I wave her off. "Nah, it's fine I'll just get Jared to come get me."

"Are you sure?" she asks. I can tell she's looking for the lie. I nod. "Yeah."

Then my phone chimes. I dig it out of my pocket and see a message from Rachel.

Rachel: @Bowl U Cming?

Rachel is there? I've hung out with her enough for one evening.

Me: Nope.
Rachel: Fine.

My mom makes her way out of the door, and after she leaves I lock the house down and head to my room. I text Adaline since she hasn't called me yet.

Me: Happy B-day <3

No response. No bubbles on the screen indicating she's even writing back to me. Nothing at all. I go through my phone and start pulling my video feeds together. I pull them up on my laptop and mix clips together. Ones from Adaline and me working in the library. Today's store adventure. The finished book nook and art center.

Once I'm finished, I watch it and make sure everything

meshed well. The clips playback, and I start to feel grumpy. Why couldn't she wait? We could have done this all together, but she had to be stubborn!

The more I watch the more pissed off I become. It's like she didn't even trust me enough to see I was going to be there. She just made up her mind that I was lazy or whatever and threw it all in my face.

Jared texts me.

```
Jared: Where are you?
Me: @home.
Jared: Y?
Me: I've got shit 2 do.
```

I probably shouldn't have said that. But the message is out there. He can yell at me later for it. I don't give a damn. I'm more concerned with Adaline. I mean, for God's sake she can't even thank me for a gift? Let alone not lie to my face and tell me she wasn't working on the project. It was her birthday and yadda yadda. Bunch of bullshit!

If I had my car, I'd drive straight over there and ask her what her problem is. I've done everything I could think to do. I mean, I gave her space and let her hang out with that moron Greg. That didn't pan out. Which hey, I'm not complaining. I rearranged my schedule in order to finish this project, and she basically craps all over it. Nothing is ever good enough.

I also got her a pair of pearl earrings because she said she always wanted them. I spent some of my savings on her, and she doesn't even bother to thank me? Well, screw her. I'm done with this bullshit.

Shit. I should probably find a way over to Foster's Park so I can take down the design on the art center we put up.

As I am getting out of my chair, there is a loud pounding on my door.

I march to the front door not even in the mood for whatever is behind it. I open it without looking and scream, "What?"

"Whoa, dude! Don't snap at me," Jared says.

"Why are you here?"

He stares at me for a minute and then Juliet comes around him and weasels her way into my house. "What the hell!" I snap.

"Sorry I have to pee! Like so bad. Which way?" she says as she does a little dance from toe to toe.

I glare at Jared for a second then let him in too. I slam the door and lock it.

Jared is following my moves as I march over to Juliet and point down the hall. "Second on the right. Don't mind the mess."

"Thanks. Oh my God, I shouldn't have drunk all the soda," she says as she rushes down the hall.

I turn to Jared. "Why are you here? I know you weren't in the neighborhood. You could have taken her to any of the gas stations in town."

He shrugs. "You done? Because I'm really pissed off at you."

"I bet. You know I've worked my ass off today, and I'm really not in the mood for a lecture." I go to the fridge and open up a bottle of water. "You want one?"

"Yeah. Thanks." He takes a bottle from me and drinks

some. "You know it's Adaline's birthday."

"I know what day it is. I also bought her a gift and stopped by her house. You think she said thank you? Nope, she just kicked me right out of her house."

I don't even hear her coming down the hall. All the sudden Juliet says, "She did? Why would she do that? She said you bailed on the project."

"She said what?" I yell. "I didn't bail on shit. She told me she wasn't working on anything because it was her birthday. She blew me off, and now she's telling people I bailed on her? Bullshit I did."

I walk into my room and snatch up my computer. I return to the living room and place my computer on the beat-up coffee table. "If I didn't do anything, why the hell did I spend all day doing this?" I push play on the tape.

Juliet and Jared go over to the couch and start watching the video. Juliet is staring at the screen with wide eyes. Jared looks dumbfounded. I'm irritated. "When did you do all this?" Juliet asks.

"I don't know, around four-ish. Why are you guys giving me that look?" I ask.

Jared shakes his head. "Dude we thought everyone on your team was blowing Addy off, so we helped her um … cheat. Sort of."

I sit down on the couch and run my hands through my hair, messing it all up. It's probably sticking out everywhere and looks like I jammed my finger in a light socket. Whatever. I look over at them and say, "She put a video together, too, didn't she?"

Juliet slowly nods. "Great!" I shout. "That's fantastic."

"You should come with us to the party," Juliet says.

"I can't," I say.

Jared shuts my laptop and says, "Why not?"

I groan. "Who's taking Ads home? You two, right? We'll drive past my old house, and she'll wonder why I'm not getting out. I can't tell anyone I live here."

"You told me," Jared mumbles.

I give him side-eyes. "Yeah, and I also said don't tell anyone, and you brought her here to use the potty."

"For what it's worth, it's nice inside," Juliet amends. "Sure, it's scary as all get out outside, but in here is nice."

"I'm never bringing Adaline here. She's too good for this dump. I just have to live here for eleven more months, then mom is moving into the city, and I'll be off at college. Hopefully," I say. "But in the meantime, no one is to know about this. Ever."

"You know Adaline won't care. She just likes you and wishes you would quit giving her the runaround," Juliet says then she slaps a hand over her mouth.

Jared leans his head back and laughs. "See, I knew you'd tell." Juliet smacks his leg, which makes him grab her hand and kiss it.

"Tell? What are you two talking about?" I ask.

Juliet sighs. "Adaline likes you. Has always liked you. But you never saw it."

"You got that table flipped. I love Adaline. I told her the next guy she was dating was going to be me. It doesn't matter, though, because she doesn't trust me. Hell, she doesn't even want to talk to me. She hasn't even opened the gift I bought her, has she?"

Juliet shakes her head. "That was from you? The one wrapped in blue paper?"

"Of course it was from me," I say.

Juliet looks at her phone for a second then says, "Shoot. We have to go."

Jared agrees. "You coming, or are you staying?" he asks.

Here is the decision time—one will leave me with a "What if?"; the other might leave me with a "What was I thinking?"

Chapter Forty-Two

Adaline

Bowling is usually fun. My best friend left with her boyfriend. I thought she said this was supposed to be my party. So shouldn't she be here celebrating with me inside of off in some crazy destination making out with her boyfriend or whatever!

I am so mad at her. Yes, she helped me with my project. I didn't need the help if she was just going to leave me here to bowl with Tyler and her sister. I like Layla and all, but she's not my best friend. Yeah, she's a twin, but that doesn't mean she can replace Juliet.

Tyler whistles while he goes to the feeder. "So, you think I can get a strike?" he asks over his shoulder.

"You won't get a strike," Layla says. She winks at me.

I have no idea what she plans on doing, but it's probably nothing good. As soon as Tyler steps through his motions and is about to release the ball, Layla yells, "Oh my God, there's a spider on you!"

Tyler drops the ball into the gutter and spins around.

"Where? Where? Get it off!"

I start chuckling. Layla is laughing hard. Tyler stops spinning and says, "Think you're so funny, don't you? I swear I'm going to get you for this."

"No, you won't. You love me," Layla says.

"I do. A lot." He walks over and kisses her. It makes me wish I wasn't here and also I had something like that.

Tyler grabs the bowling ball and goes again. This time he only knocks down seven pins, though.

"Dang it!" he growls.

Layla skips past him. "I told you I was going to beat you."

Tyler slumps down in the seat across from me and says, "Why so glum, Addy? You know they just went to get your cupcakes. Juliet forgot them at her house."

"I know Juliet. She never forgets anything. So, nice try."

He shrugs. "All right, it was really Jared's fault. He was supposed to grab them. She was throwing lots of shade his way. So he said they'd go back and get them."

Layla bowls and hits nearly all the pins. Three are up. She points at Tyler. "Ha. In your face!"

"Babe, don't go rubbing it in," Tyler says.

"I don't even like cupcakes," I grumble. I love brownies. Juliet knows this.

"What was that?" Tyler asks.

I shake my head. "Nothing." This is officially the worst birthday ever!

The first game is still going on, and I just want to go home. As I'm about to call one of my parents, Juliet rushes over to me and wraps her arms around me. I scowl at her. No amount of hugs is going to make up for the crap she put me through.

"I'm leaving," I say.

"You can't leave. I mean, you can, but please don't. I have a surprise," she says.

I would love to tell my best friend where she can stick that surprise. I'm in a bad mood, and this shouldn't happen on my birthday. It is, though, and the fact my best friend put me in this mood makes me question our friendship.

"Addy, come on. I promise it was worth the wait," she says.

I highly doubt it. Unless this so-called surprise is a time machine, then yes, I very much doubt it. She drags me over to Jared, and this just infuriates me. "My surprise is your boyfriend? I'm leaving, right now."

"No. Not Jared."

Austin steps out and hands me some brownies. I glare at all of them. The brownies, him, my best friend, and her boyfriend. I cannot believe out of all the things to surprise me with, she chose Austin and some brownies. "You're not happy," Juliet says with a frown.

"Of course I'm not. Like, why would you bring him here and think that's supposed to make me happy?" I turn to Austin. "I should kick you in the shin."

Austin sets the tray of brownies down on a table next to us. His eyes find mine then he snaps, "You think I'm happy with you right now? I'm not. I give you a gift. You can't even thank me. I see that you did the project without me, too, by the way. That's okay, though, because the rest of the group did a project too."

Jared pipes in, "We're going to be over there starting a new game. You two can join whenever you want." He guides Juliet away from Austin and me.

I glance over at the brownies. I grab one and shove it right into Austin's face. He blinks a few times and then proceeds to wipe the chocolate mess from his face. "I cannot believe you did that," he growls.

I place my hands on my hips. "Well, I did. What are you going to do about it?"

He snatches a brownie and does the same thing to my face. I'm in shock, but I'm also laughing. I don't even know why; this isn't even funny.

"Damn it, Ads. I love the hell out of you. But when you told me not to worry about the project, I assumed you wanted to start on it tomorrow, but it turns out you just had to be stubborn."

"I'm leaving for Paris in five days."

"For spring break, right?"

I shrug. "Could be longer. I could transfer everything over and just stay there at my aunt's."

Austin shakes his head. "Don't. Please, I'll do anything, but please don't go."

"Why?"

He grabs my arms and pulls me over to a bench and kneels in front of me, chocolate still smeared on his face. "Did you not hear me when I said I love the hell out of you? Because I do, Adaline Bea. I love your scrunched nose. I love how your hair is like sunshine. I love how well you really know me."

"But … you said nothing was going on with us."

"I know what I said. It came out all wrong. There is something with us. It's not official because I never asked you. But there is something, and I'm just going to get it out there. Adaline, go out with me."

I stare at him. I feel his hands on mine. I see him, hear his intake of breaths. But this can't be real. "If you feel like this, why have you shoved me away?"

He looks down and then back at me. A deep sigh escapes him. "You deserve better than me. I can't give you crap you deserve. I want to. Believe me, I want to, but shit, I'm poor as hell. I live in a dump. Don't look at me like that."

"Like what?"

"Like I'm a kicked animal. I'm not telling you this for pity. I am telling you this because you need to know. I won't be able to come pick you up every day as I may want because we only have one car, and you've been in it. My dad left, and things went downhill. When football rolls around again, I'm going to be working hard. Basketball, same thing. And there won't be much time between that, school, and work for you. I need you to get all that. I have to work. I have to play sports. It's my only way to school. If you're down with that, I want to give this a try."

I squeeze his hands. "You didn't ask me out because you're poor?"

"Yeah. Something like that."

"Am I really that arrogant?" I ask and shove his hands off my lap.

He backs up and stands. "No. What? No."

I stand up, too, and try to create some distance between us. "I swear you don't know me at all. I only wanted you." I take off out the doors and dial my mom. I keep walking away from the building, so if anyone comes out looking for me, they won't be able to pull me back inside. How did my birthday turn into such a crap day?

Chapter Forty-Three

Austin

This is why I never wanted to tell her anything. Juliet and Jared convinced me to, and it's nothing but a slap in my face. The girl hates the hell out of me now.

I glare at my friends.

Tyler shakes his head. "Dude, why didn't you tell me? I thought this whole time you had gambling issues."

"Shut up! I didn't tell you because you didn't need to know. You all have perfect lives. Mine turned to shit!"

Juliet and Jared say nothing, but Layla isn't quiet. "You think we have perfect lives? Juliet and I had to watch our mom basically fall into a depression and then open a matchmaking business. For years she fed people a bullshit line that happiness was a phone call away. But she wasn't happy. We all have our shit to deal with. But friends make it better."

I look over at Tyler. A simple warning he better get hold of his girl. I'm not in the mood. "Look, you might not wanna hear it, but Layla is right. We all have shit. My parents suck. Jared's dad is a total dick. Their mom is cool, but she relies on them to do a lot," Tyler says while flitting a look over at Juliet and Layla. "Sure we have the housing stability, but bro, you can't let that hold you back. You like Addy, then go after her. Don't sit here and wait around."

"Make a grand gesture," Juliet says. "We love grand gestures."

"I made one, at the park. She didn't see it yet," I snap.

Jared slaps the seat next to him. "Then you better find her and show her."

He tosses me his truck keys. "Don't wreck it," he says as I catch them.

I cannot believe this is happening. I leave the bowling alley and get into Jared's truck. I hate manuals, by the way, hate them. While I'm changing gears, I'm cursing. I drive down the street; she has to be on her way to her house. I hope I'm wrong and she's at a bench or something.

In the distance, I spot her. I pull up alongside her and roll down the passenger window. "Get in."

"My mom is coming. Did you steal Jared's truck?"

"No. Get in. Please, Adaline. If you don't, I'll follow you home and tell your parents we have to complete a homework assignment and you've been avoiding me."

Her eyes widen. "You would not."

"I will. I have nothing left to lose."

She scowls. "Fine. I need to talk to my mom. She's on her way."

"Get in then, and call her. I'll take you back if you want."

She nods and dials her mom. "Hi. Sorry. I found Austin,

and he said he would take me home." There is a pause, and then she says, "Yes. I know. Love you too." She hangs up and looks over at me. "Fine. She wasn't really on her way I called her like ten seconds before you got here."

"Good. Buckle up."

"Do you even know how to drive this thing?"

I shrug. "I'm rusty, but I know."

She peers over at me. "So there is a good chance of us dying?"

"Sunshine, there is always a chance of us dying."

"That's not reassuring at all."

I watch her strap in, then I move us away from the curb. "It'll be fine," I say.

I don't look over at her anymore because I need to concentrate. I'm glad Jared's dad taught Tyler, Jared, and me how to drive Jared's truck. Otherwise, we would be screwed.

"Where are we going?" she asks.

"The park."

She groans. "I don't want to have a reminder of why I'm mad at you, Austin."

"Who said it would be a reminder of why you're mad? You just assume it will be. So, stop assuming and start trusting."

I drive us over to the park, but I'm not close enough that we can see the book nook, so I tell her, "Shut your eyes."

"I'm not doing that."

"Please. Come on. You kind of owe me. Rubbing brownie in my face, running away, not talking to me, not thanking me for your gift, do you want me to go on? I have plenty others," I tease.

She slaps my arm. "All right. I'll shut my eyes. If you lead me to a pond, I'm beating you up."

"I promise not lead you to water, or your death."

She gives me a look but shuts her eyes. "You'll have to get me out of the truck."

I put Jared's truck in park, make my way over to her side, and help her out. Her soft hands grip mine, and I love every minute of it. I guide her over to the area where our projects are and say, "Okay, open."

Chapter Forty-Four

Adaline

I open my eyes, and in front of me is not only the project I did but a huge colored wall. On the wall written in what looks to be chalk says, "Adaline, will you go out with me?"

"What the heck?"

"When we got here today, I was super ticked off because you already made and put up our original project. So, I decided to put up a project too. Consider it an extra combo if you will."

I point at the sign. "You wrote that?" I ask.

"Yeah. Everyone saw it. Most of the group ragged on me for it, but I don't care. I'm dead serious."

My heart races. I want to blurt out "Yes." I can't believe he did all this for me. But there is something holding me back. "Rachel saw this?"

He nods. "Yes, Adaline, Rachel saw this. Who cares?"

Tears slip from my eyes, and I say, "Okay."

"Okay, what?"

"I will go out with you," I say. "It has to be after we turn in our project. Please tell me you made a video."

He kisses my lips and then laughs. "Of course I made one. What do you take me for?"

Relief washes over me. All kinds because I wasn't sure how my video would have panned out. I have clips of Zander and Lucas napping in our meetings. I have Rachel tapping away on her phone but looking extremely annoyed. I have a few of Austin and me collaborating, but it looked like crap. There I admit it—we would have failed, hands down.

The next morning Austin and I are sitting in my kitchen piecing together each bit of video feed. My mom is staring at us most of the time. Austin doesn't say anything, but it is getting to me. "Mom, what do you want?"

"I was wondering how long this has been going on?"

I look over at Austin then back at my mom. "What? Us working together? I told you I had a few projects due before break."

"No. I mean how long have you two been a thing?" she asks, completely embarrassing me.

Austin laughs. "Well, it wasn't for a lack of trying to get this one to agree on a date with me, but as of yesterday." He nudges me, and I shake my head.

My mom smiles. "I'm glad you made him work for it." She throws in a wink then says, "You two staying for dinner?"

"I'd love to, Mrs. Frost, but I gotta pick my mom up after her shift is done. Rain check?"

"Okay. Austin, remind me, what did your mom do at the hospital?" she asks.

He blanches. "She was head of the scheduling department for all the O. R."

"Hmmm, have her give me a call. I might have something up her alley."

She slides him a business card, and Austin salutes her. "Will do."

Once she's out of the kitchen, I take a deep breath and exhale. "I thought she was never leaving," I say.

"Yeah, why? Did you want to do something naughty to me?"

I giggle. "No." I grab his face and kiss him. "I didn't want to do that with my mom watching."

Austin chuckles. "Yeah, no PDA in front of the parents. How does this look so far?" He hits play on his screen, and our entire video plays back to us.

"I think this is A worthy."

And it totally was.

THE END

Acknowledgments

I'm grateful and blessed by the support from all you amazing readers. Thank you for being a part of this awesome journey with me. Each one of you holds a special place in my heart, for I know without you, none of this would even be possible. Thank you so much!

To my truly fantastic family and my two incredibly-amazing children, you inspire me to be the very best version of myself. When I'm frustrated, you push me to do better, make me laugh, and are always there encouraging me each and every day. I love you so much.

To my kick-ass agent, Brittany Booker, you are awesome! Your advice makes my writing better. Thank you so much for your insight!

To my most-amazing publisher, Georgia McBride, thank you so much for believing in my book! You are a rock star inside and out. Without you, this wouldn't be possible. Thank you so much for all you do. I'm truly thankful to be a part of this wonderful imprint!

My friends, fellow writers, and CP's, without you, I don't think I could have gotten through some days. You're always in my corner listening to my frustrations and help my work shine even more. Thank you for being my eyes and ears. You all are fantastic!

My phenomenal peeps in EL!T3, thank you for the escape. You all make me laugh when I really want to throw my computer out the window. I love our chats and when we kick some serious butt. Love you all!

Of course, I can't forget the wonderful and super amazing staff at Swoon Romance. You all rock! Keep doing what you are doing. Total love for all of you!

Special thanks to: Ethan, Leeah, Jason, Brittany Booker, Josie Glauser, Tracey Chapman, Angie Ball, Clarissa Grimes, Georgia McBride, Staci Cranor, Justin Whitehead, Julie Sykes, Sheri Larsen, Michelle Aker, Maggie Adams, and Bria Quinlan.

Natalie Decker

Natalie Decker is the author of the bestselling YA series *Rival Love*, bestselling YA series *Offsides,* and bestselling NA series *Scandalous Boys*. She loves her family, awesome dog, and friends. She enjoys carefree days, football, fuzzy blankets, traveling, reading, cooking, writing, and is a huge Denver Broncos fan. Her imagination is always active. She believes in seeing the world in a different light at all times and is an avid reader of everything. If she's not at a Target or Starbucks, she might be typing away on her laptop, reading a book, hanging out with her amazing family, or off having an adventure. Because Natalie believes in saying: *Your life is a journey, so make it amazing!*

Natalie loves interacting with readers. Feel free to follow her on any of her social media accounts. If you would like a chance to get exclusive material & ARCs visit her website: www.authornataliedecker.com and sign up for her mailing list. No spam or unsolicited materials will be sent.

OTHER SWOON ROMANCE TITLES YOU MIGHT LIKE

RIGHT TEXT WRONG NUMBER
RIGHT KISS WRONG GUY

Find more books like this at http://www.myswoonromance.com

Connect with Swoon Romance online:
Facebook: https://www.Facebook.com/swoonromance
Instagram: http://www.instagram.com/swoonromance
Twitter: https://twitter.com/SwoonRomance
Tumblr: http://swoonromance.tumblr.com/
Georgia McBride Media Group: www.georgiamcbride.com

Right Text Wrong Number

Offsides Book One

Author of the Rival Love Series

Natalie Decker

RIGHT KISS
WRONG GUY

OFFSIDES BOOK TWO

AUTHOR OF THE RIVAL LOVE SERIES
NATALIE DECKER